THE
AUTUMN
DEAD

Other titles in the Allison & Busby American Crime series

THE
AUTUMN
DEAD

Ed Gorman

Allison & Busby
Published by W.H. Allen & Co. Plc

An Allison & Busby book
Published in 1989 by
W.H. Allen & Co. Plc
44 Hill Street
London W1X 8LB

First published in the USA
by St Martin's Press

Copyright © 1987 by Ed Gorman

Printed and bound in Great Britain by
Anchor Brendon Ltd, Tiptree, Essex

ISBN 0 85031 974 9 (hardback edition)
ISBN 0 85031 964 1 (paperback edition)

For my wife Carol,
abiding love.

Night, the shadow of light,
And life, the shadow of death.

—ALGERNON CHARLES SWINBURNE

1 I spent two hours that rainy Tuesday morning honoring my boss's request to explain to a chunky twenty-two-year-old Chicano kid named Diaz why he'd get canned if he ever again used the choke hold on anybody.

"He was shoplifting, man," Diaz said.

"Not exactly the same as shooting or raping somebody."

"He looked dangerous."

"He's forty-three years old and he gets early social security because he shakes so bad from injuries he picked up in Nam. I saw him, Diaz. The poor bastard's barely alive. He shoplifts because the boys in Washington cut vets' benefits. And in his present condition, he couldn't whip Madonna." I lost it then, just a bit. "We're rent-a-cops, Diaz. We're not mercenaries or whatever those guys are in those magazines you read. You understand?"

Diaz has an annoying habit of snuffling phlegm up in his throat, then expectorating it into his empty Styrofoam coffee cup. I have to wait a few hours afterward before I can even think about eating again. He did it now and he kept his eyes on me all the time he was doing it. "I ain't gonna get wasted because of some weirdo creep, man. The boss don't let us carry iron, then he shouldn't have no objections when we use some force."

Carry iron. Inside his head, Diaz, like too many other rent-a-cops who can't get jobs as real policemen, lives out scenes from grade-B action movies. Carry iron. How about just saying "go armed"? But Charles Bronson would never put it that way, now would he? "Sometimes you have to use force, but not on somebody who's barely alive, and not the choke hold. Unless it's life and death, and it's rarely life and death."

He wiped his hands on the front of his uniform shirt. The American Security uniform is light blue with dark blue epaulets and fine gold buttons. It makes us look like cops who moonlight as bus drivers.

"I put up with this shit for minimum wage, man," Diaz said. He might have been nice-looking if he lost twenty-five pounds and did something about his zits and smiled. I'd seen him smile only once in the three months he'd worked here. That was the time Hanrahan, another rent-a-cop, told about the time he'd busted a shoplifter's arm. Hanrahan and Diaz swapped issues of mercenary magazines. Diaz, inhaling a Winston, said now, "I should at least be able to have a little fun."

He knew he'd really get me going with that one and I was all ready to let go, but then the intercom started crackling in the small back room with the Pepsi machine and the sandwich machine and the trash barrel that gets emptied only when the well-fed cockroaches join hands and start dancing around it. Poker gets played a lot back there, and according to legend, a very beautiful rent-a-cop named Stephanie did it with a rent-a-cop named Ken right on the table. To me that tale sounds like something out of one of Diaz's magazines.

"Dwyer?" Bobby Lee said.

"Yes?"

"Somebody here to see you."

"Can he wait a bit?"

"It isn't a he. It's a she." She explained this with a modest hint of disapproval. She and Donna have become good friends, and when Donna's not around, Bobby Lee acts as her surrogate home-room monitor.

"She give her name?"

"Yes. Karen Lane."

So there you have it.

I'm standing here in my para—bus driver uniform, forty-four years of age, ten pounds overweight, spending part of my time cuffing shoplifters and the other picking up small bits as an actor of dubious talent, not exactly what you'd call the American success story, and Karen Lane comes back into my life.

Twenty-five years ago Karen Lane, who then bore an unnerving resemblance to Natalie Wood, had broken not only my heart but my bank account. Even though we were both from the same poor neighborhood, the Highlands, Karen had early on gotten used to the pleasures to be had merely by smiling. Rich boys had been lining up for her ever since she'd first strolled onto a playground; I had never been sure how I'd gotten in that line, even if it had been only for a few months.

The odd thing was that no matter how many years passed, the stray thought came back once or twice a year that someday I'd run into her again, though of course in a lurid soap-opera fashion. I'd be an established actor by then and Karen would be this smiled-out hag with six kids and a husband who beat her as often as he had the strength left over from his job in the coal mines.

So there you have it.

She doesn't have the grace to wait till you're living in Hollywood and hanging around with Jimmy Garner and Bob Redford, uh-uh, she comes back some rainy Tuesday morning when you're chewing out some fleshy bullyboy who enjoys choking some poor vet who has to resort to stealing because he's broke.

"You look weird, man," Diaz said.

"Huh?"

"Weird. Your face."

"Yeah?"

"Yeah." He nodded to the intercom. "This lady, this Karen Lane broad, she must be special, huh?"

"Not the way you mean."

"Bitch, huh?"

I shrugged. "Used to be. Maybe she's changed."

"I knew a bitch once." He made a fist. Showed it to me the way most men would show you pictures of their babies. "She answered to Papa." He always called his fist Papa.

"Diaz," I said, but what was the use?

"What?"

"I know your situation."

"What situation?"

"Your home situation, asshole."

"Oh, yeah."

"Your mother couldn't get by without your paycheck. And this would be the third job you've lost in six months. So cool it with the John Wayne crap, all right?"

I was starting to feel sorry for him—his life wasn't without frustration, he had six brothers and sisters still of school age, and a mother too haggard to work and a father who had died of heart disease three months ago—but it was dangerous to feel sorry for Diaz because he'd kill you with your pity. He'd put you to the wall with your pity.

I said, "You get the impulse to put the choke hold on somebody, try to think of your mother, okay?"

"What you think I am, man, some kind of fruit?"

I sighed and shook my head.

He picked up his Styrofoam coffee and snuffled some phlegm into it. Then he held the cup out to me. "You thirsty, man?"

On the way down the hall, Robbins, the boss, stopped me. He's a big man, six-five, and the proud possessor of the world's largest collection of clip-on neckties. "Holy moley, Dwyer." He still says that. Holy moley.

"What?"

"That babe."

"Oh, yeah."

He smiled. He'd just gotten a haircut and there were white wiry flecks of hair all over his shoulders. He smelled of the kind of sweet hair tonic my father's barber had always used on all the working guys. Sweet enough to kill a chocolate urge. "'Oh, yeah.' Real casual like." He jabbed at my chest with a plump finger. "Donna's gonna kick your ass when she finds out."

"Robbins, honest, I haven't seen this woman in twenty-five years."

"Right," he said and winked. He had a wink like my uncle Phil, whom I once saw trying to peek in the women's john at a family reunion. He winked because he likes me and considers us friends, and I like him fine and I consider him a friend, too, if only because we are the only people in the agency who've actually been real cops. "You should keep me filled in on this stuff, Dwyer." Then he put a Tiparillo in his mouth and strolled off down the hall to his office.

All his talk about how good-looking Karen Lane was caused me to lean into the john, grind a comb through hair getting steely with gray, and make sure my teeth didn't have samples of my breakfast still stuck in the cracks. I stood there and looked at myself and then shrugged. I wasn't magically going to get any better looking.

So I went out to the lobby where Robbins, for reasons I've never actually understood, has arrayed blown-up black-and-white photos of criminals ranging from Jesse James to a guy he calls Lefty Dalwoski, who, he claims, was such a despicable bastard that he not only shot a nun but shot her in the back. "Christ," he always said, "at least if he'd shot her in the front, she'd have had a chance." What chance? To draw her Magnum? What order of nuns go armed—the Sisters of the Holy Luger?

In addition to the rogues gallery, there is enough cheap furniture to fill a small house: two coffee tables, four overstuffed chairs (one of which is honest-to-God paisley), and a lime-green couch that looks as if a pyromaniac used to work it over with cigarettes right after the kitties got done using it as a litter box. Robbins used to be in the loan-collection business, and what he couldn't get in cash, he took in furniture. "You need anything," he always says, "let me know. I got this warehouse full of shit." And shit it was, too.

In the center of the reception area sits another one of Robbins' catches, a desk big enough to play Ping-Pong on. This he got from a banker who'd embezzled several hundred thousand for the sake of a nineteen-year-old teller who wore falsies on her breasts and braces on her teeth. Robbins got these details from the coroner. The banker, trapped, killed himself and the girl. The banker had owed a loan company money (go figure) and Robbins had been dispatched to collect it. As usual on debts he couldn't collect, he took furniture.

Anyway, the desk is usually occupied by a woman whose breasts have inspired as many hours of conversation as the sins of Richard Nixon. Her name is Bobby Lee, and she is maybe forty (who would dare ask?) and she is the kind of woman who breaks into tears at the mere mention of Elvis Presley's name. Indeed, once a year she and her 1965 beehive hairdo and her mother and father drive in their motorhome to Graceland where, Bobby Lee claims, she once heard Elvis himself speak to her From Beyond The Grave. When she told me this, I asked, with at least a tad of condescension, "What did he say to you?" And she'd looked generally shocked. "God, Dwyer, that's personal. All I'll say is that it made me feel much better." Anyway, Bobby Lee and I had not gotten along until the last year or so, mostly due to her previously having been the mistress of my former employer, an anal retentive who runs a security agency the way wardens run death rows. The man had dumped Bobby Lee and in so doing had sent her running back to her Baptist faith, which she now espoused with the fervor of Saint Paul in a debating contest. Having her heart broken had turned her not only religious but human, too, so when the guy fired her, I got her a job over here.

Now she sat in the reception area and answered the phones and smoked enough Kool filters to give an entire stadium lung cancer and dispatched American Security people with the curt competence of old George Patton sending men into battle.

But it wasn't Bobby Lee I was looking at now. It was this beautiful five-five woman with dazzling auburn hair touching the shoulders of her white cashmere sweater and her hands tucked gracefully into the pockets of her white pleated trousers. She was as tan as a travel poster and benumbing as the first moment you ever fell in love.

As she raised her clean blue gaze to mine, I realized that Karen Lane had managed the impossible. She not

7

only looked as good as she had twenty-five years ago—she looked better.

"Hi, Jack."

"Hi."

"I'll bet you're surprised to see me."

"Not any more surprised than I'd be if the Pope called me for lunch."

She laughed. She had a wonderful laugh. I wanted to dive in it and drown. "Still a smart-ass."

Bobby Lee took the Kool from the corner of her mouth and said, "That's what his girlfriend Donna always says. What a smart-ass he is." She scowled at me.

"Oh, so he has a girlfriend?" Karen said, picking up on the point Bobby Lee had wanted to make. She didn't take her beautiful eyes from me. Not for a moment.

"Yes, he most certainly does."

"Do you think she'd mind if I asked Jack to lunch?" And her eyes were still on mine.

"I wouldn't think a real lady would need to ask a question like that," Bobby Lee said and put her fake Fu Manchu fingernails to the keyboard, blocking us out with Zen mastery.

And then Karen laughed again and for the first time let her eyes fall on Bobby Lee. "I'm sorry. I probably am coming on a little strong, aren't I? I'm actually here to see Jack on business."

Bobby Lee of course said nothing. But she exhaled in such a way that you could see how each and every fiber in her T-shirt strained against the overabundance of her breasts. Her T-shirts always had pictures of country-music stars on them. Today Willy Nelson had the pleasure of being buoyed on her bust.

"So how about it, Jack?" Karen Lane said. "Some lunch? On me?"

8

I looked at Bobby Lee. "I better ask my mom here first."

"Very funny," Bobby Lee said, then turned around again and started tapping on her Wang keyboard.

So Karen Lane and I left the building and went down to the curb to get her car. It was new and it was dazzling white and it was every inch a Jaguar sedan.

2 The nuns who'd taught us would not have been proud of her.

On the way to the Harcourt, a restaurant I could afford to eat at only if I'd recently stuck up a 7-Eleven, she gave me some sense of what she'd been doing during the twenty-five years since we'd graduated from St. Michael's.

There had been four husbands. She did not describe them in emotional terms—"great guy" or "wonderful lover" or "wife beater"—instead I got their occupations and some sense of their financial status.

Number One was an "internist who lost a lot when the Market got soft in the early seventies." Two was an AFL linebacker who'd been "very content to take early retirement and start his own insurance agency in Decatur, Illinois." Three was curator of an art museum and he was "all inherited money the bulk of which he wouldn't come into until he turned fifty and he was only twenty-nine." Four was a communications magnate "who took a big gamble on buying up indepen-

9

dent TV stations and then really lost big when cable came in."

Then there were the places she'd lived: Los Angeles ("I've never felt lonelier"); Ft. Lauderdale ("If you've got enough money, you can pretend it's sixteenth-century Florence"); Denver ("No matter how rich they are there, they've all got cow shit on their shoes"); Paris ("No matter what they say to the contrary, their noses are much bigger than their cocks, believe me"); and New York ("From my window I could look over Central Park and I felt just like Holly Golightly.")

It was when she said the last that I stopped her. "Can I ask you a question?"

"Sure."

"Is this on tape?"

She laughed her wonderful laugh. "God, I really am talking a lot, aren't I?"

"Then can I ask you another question?"

"What?"

"Who is Holly Golightly?"

"Didn't you ever read *Breakfast at Tiffany's* by Truman Capote?"

"I read *In Cold Blood.* It was great."

She frowned. "I started it, but it was too depressing. But *Breakfast at Tiffany's*—you know, we were in high school when that came out and one Saturday I went downtown to the library to pick up a book and I chose that one because, frankly, I've never been much of a reader and because it was very thin and the type was very big and there was this really fascinating photograph of Capote on the back. And so I took it home and read it and it changed my life. It really did. I mean, it really inspired me. I wanted to be just like Holly Golightly. Then after graduation I took the two hundred dollars I'd saved from my summer job and went down to the bus depot and got a Greyhound and headed straight for New York. God, it was fantastic."

And I heard then what I should have heard—and understood—back when I was twenty and hoping my frail hopes that she'd somehow fall in love with me: That something central was missing in her—my old man would have called it horse sense—that she was as giddy and unlikely and impossible as any tale ever told in the pages of *Modern Screen.*

But where most women gave up such dreams under the press of eight-to-five jobs or infants who demanded tits and taters or husbands who made it their business to crush every little hope their wives ever had—Karen Lane had had the sheer beauty and the sheer deranged gall to pursue her particular muses.

That was why, even back in grade school, she'd scared me. She was some kind of combination of Audrey Hepburn and Benito Mussolini.

Then we were sitting at a stoplight, a laundry truck on one side of us, a school bus on the other, and she leaned over and before I knew what was happening, she threw her arms around me and put her tongue, with the precision of a surgical instrument, right inside my mouth.

I could tell when the light changed because the cars behind us started honking and the drivers yelling.

She was soft and tasted great and I was trembling and feeling one of those erections you're only supposed to get when you're sixteen and every bit as daffy, at least at the moment, as she was.

Then, bowing to the authority of horns and curses, she took herself away from me, and I felt as deserted as an orphan.

But before she went back to driving, she patted me on the knee in an oddly cool, almost matronly way and

11

said, "I know you're going to help me, Jack. I just know it."

The east end of the Harcourt sits on a promontory over a lake lost that day in fog and rain. Somewhere in the distance big wooden workboats moved like massive prehistoric animals through haze that blanched everything of colors. Everything looked and felt gray on this March day.

On this side of the vast curved window a waiter who seemed to have watched an awful lot of Charles Boyer movies was making a fool of himself over Karen while trying to keep up a French accent that was falling down like socks that had lost their elastic.

"Ze braised fresh carb claws," he said and rolled his eyes the way he probably did during sex.

"They sound wonderful. Just wonderful." And then she smiled over at me. "Don't they sound wonderful, Jack?"

"'Wonderful' isn't the word for it," I said.

"And ze sautéed fresh prawns with shredded ham and vegetables." He rolled his eyes again. I had decided that if he managed to work "ooh-là-là" into the conversation, I was going to deck him.

While he finished flirting with Karen, I glanced around the Harcourt and knew again that my speed was Hardees. Here you sat on English walnut chairs and stared at paintings by Matisse (whom I happened to like in my uneducated way) and large blow-ups of Cartier-Bresson photographs (which I thought I could probably duplicate with my Polaroid) and ate with forks that weighed two and a half pounds and daubed goose-liver pâté off your lips with brilliant white napkins big enough to double as sheets.

When the waiter finally packed up his French accent and went away, Karen said, "You look uncomfortable."

I sighed. "Can I be honest?"

"Of course. Honesty is something I really value."

I tried not to be uncharitable, but I couldn't keep the hard cold trust-department way she'd assessed her husbands out of my mind. If that was her idea of honesty, then maybe I would have preferred her a bit dishonest.

"Your father," I said.

She looked perplexed. "What about him?"

"He lived in the Highlands, right?"

"Why, yes. Of course."

"The Highlands being the area in this city with the lowest per-capita income and the highest crime rate."

"What's the point, Jack?" Irritation had come into her voice.

"That's where your father was from and my father was from and that's where you're from and that's where I'm from."

"Would you please come to the point?"

"I'm ashamed of you, that's the point."

"What?" She sat back in her chair as if I'd just tried to slap her.

"You've bought into an awful lot of bullshit, you know that? New white Jaguars and measuring people by their bank accounts and indulging silly assholes like that waiter."

"Are you drunk?"

"No."

"Are you on drugs?"

"No."

"Then you have absolutely no right to speak to me that way."

"Sure I do. I've known you since you were six years old and we made our First Communion together and you were always full of shit, Karen, but you've never been *this* full of shit before."

So—what else?—she started crying.

There were approximately three hundred other people in the big restaurant, most of them men and most
of them with gold American Express cards pulsating in
their suits, and now nearly every one of them was staring at us.

If she was faking, she was good at it because she
didn't go for any big sobs or anything like that, she just
sat there and put her beautiful head into one beautiful
hand and small tears rolled down her beautiful cheeks
and touched her beautiful red glossy lips.

"I overdid it," I said.

She just kept her head down.

I looked out at the fog and the wooden workboats
and the hint of birch-lined shore somewhere in the
haze.

I said, "I said I overdid it."

She looked up. "Is that supposed to be an apology?"

"About half an apology."

"I want and deserve more than half an apology."

"Your old man worked with my old man in the same
factory. They had Spam for lunch and they played pinochle every Friday night, and even if they weren't
smart and they weren't important, they knew enough
to hate bullshit. And that's all you seem to know,
Karen. Bullshit."

"Well, thank you very much."

Our positions had shifted subtly here. Her tears had
dried and I was angry again. "You're welcome."

So we sat in uncomfortable silence for a time.

"You're making a lot of assumptions about me, Jack."

"Sure."

"You are. How do you know that I haven't had a lot
of pain in my life?"

"You mean in between having your accountant going
through your husband's bank account so you can decide if he's worth keeping or not."

14

"There was a perfectly good reason for each divorce."

"Right."

"Incompatibility."

She said it so fecklessly that it had an odd endearing quality. "Incompatibility? That's legalese, Karen. More bullshit. It's meaningless."

"Well, whether you choose to believe it or not, I was incompatible with each and every one of my husbands for a very simple reason. Because I wanted to find myself and they didn't want me to."

"Finding yourself went out in the seventies, Karen, along with earth shoes."

For the first time, she sulked, beautiful as always but looking a bit trapped now. "Anyway, Jack, two can play the honesty game."

"Meaning what?"

"Meaning that I know very well why you're being so mean."

"Why?"

"Because of that night I took your car."

Actually, of all her many betrayals, that had been one that had slipped my mind. Now, though, instead of inspiring pain, it caused me to laugh. It was that outrageous. "I forgot all about that. You said you needed to borrow my car so you could help your mother with grocery shopping because your family car was getting fixed. And then you took my goddamn car—that I'd worked my ass off to buy—and you took Larry Price to the drive-in in it."

She leaned forward and pursed her lips as if she was getting impatient with my misunderstanding of her. "Well, for your information, even if I did use your car to take Larry to the drive-in, it wasn't what you think. The drive-in was just a good place to talk."

"Right."

I sensed but could not define something shift in her gaze. Ever since we'd started talking about Larry Price, her jaw had set and a strange anger was in her eyes.

But I was too concerned with my own anger to worry about hers. I was almost overwhelmed with the purity of my rage even though twenty-five years had passed. "Larry Price, Ted Forester, David Haskins—you knew how I hated them. And you know why, too. What they did to Malley and me that night."

Price, Forester, and Haskins had been seniors when we'd been juniors. One night they'd depantsed a wimpy kid everybody picked on with the casual cruelty of young people who constantly needed to reassure themselves they were normal and cool and slick. Then they'd beaten him and beaten him badly. And it so happened that when Malley and I heard about it, we got a six-pack and sat around and talked about it a lot, kind of working ourselves up, and then we went looking for them. And it was all supposed to go our way because we were righteous and we were poor, and poor kids were supposed to be tough, but when we found them, it didn't work out that way at all. Even though Price and Forester and Haskins had only come to St. Michael's in a redistricting of Catholic schools and did not socially fit in—they were the sons of very wealthy and successful people—they were at least one thing they were not supposed to be, and that was tough. My friend fought Forester and did not do well at all, and then I fought Price and did even less well. For weeks we tried to explain that to each other—"You know, if we hadn't been so drunk, man, there wouldn't have been nothing left of those guys"—but it was all bull and we hadn't been tough enough, and that remained, even today, a source of secret shame.

So five weeks later, my supposed girlfriend Karen

Lane borrows my car and takes Larry Price to the drive-in.

"Maybe it wasn't what you think, Jack."

"Sure."

I was about to say more, coasting on my anger now, when she pulled something up from her lap and set it on the table next to the fresh-cut rose in the slender vase.

A white envelope.

"Money," she said.

"For what?"

"That isn't the question you should be asking first."

"What question should I be asking first?"

"You should be more curious about how much there is than what it's for."

"So how much is there?"

"A thousand dollars."

"I'm impressed."

"You should be. I'm practically broke."

"Now I want to know what it's for."

"Because I want you to do me a favor."

"I've already got doubts."

"It's perfectly legal."

"Right."

"All it involves is you getting back something that belongs to me."

"And what would that be?"

"A suitcase."

"Where is it?"

"In a condo on the northeast edge of the city."

"And who lives in the condo?"

"A man named Evans. Glendon Evans."

"Glendon?"

"That's his full name. But everybody calls him Glen. Including his patients."

"Patients?"

"He's a psychiatrist."

"I see." I sipped some water. "Why can't you just call Glendon or Glen and ask him if you can have your suitcase?"

"I'm afraid he's angry with me."

"Ah."

"What does that mean?"

"It means that I sense *amore* is somehow involved. True?"

"We lived together nearly a year."

"But now you want out?"

"I am out and have been out for a month, but he won't give me my suitcase back."

"Where are you staying now?"

"Do you remember Susan Roberts?"

"Sure." Susan had been a slight but lovely girl, given, unlike most of us in the Highlands, to things of culture and beauty. You never found Susan at the drag strip on Sunday afternoons. She had also been, as I recalled, obsessive about a guy named Gary Roberts whose sole desire had been to be a writer.

"She married Gary. Did you know that?"

"Yes," I said.

"He's a teacher. A very good one." She smiled. "And he still writes. Every day. And someday, he'll get something published. You wait and see."

"You're apologizing for him. That's arrogant. He's probably a lot happier than these jack-offs you've been married to."

"Would you please just not be so angry?"

I sighed. "You're right. I'm being angry and I'm being arrogant and now I'll apologize."

"I appreciate it."

"So you've been staying with the Robertses?"

"Yes. They were the ones who told me that you'd been a policeman and now were a private investigator."

"Mostly I bust shoplifters."

Now she sipped her water. "But certainly you have enough experience to get my suitcase back."

"What's so special about it?"

"It's just got a lot of sentimental things in it."

Which I didn't believe at all. She struck me about as sentimental as Charles Manson's sister. But I let it pass. "And the suitcase is in the condo?"

"Yes."

"So if I went in there and got it for you, I'd be committing B and E."

"B and E?"

"Breaking and entering."

"Not really."

"Why not?"

"First, because the suitcase belongs to me, and second, because I have a key."

Which she produced with a distinct air of *voilà*. Even in the blanched light of the gray day, she still looked tan and overpoweringly lovely.

"Did you know there's a reunion dance tonight?" she said.

"I know. Number twenty-five. I'm not going."

"Why?"

"Because I feel old enough already. I don't need to confirm my suspicions by looking at people with bald heads and potbellies and wattles like turkeys. I've got all that stuff myself."

"Actually, Jack, you're still very handsome in your way."

"You always said that, that 'in my way' thing, and it always bothered me."

"Well, you're not Robert Redford, but you're appealing. You really are."

"So what about the reunion?"

"Well, I thought it would be fun if you just kind of

popped over this afternoon and got my suitcase and then popped over to the reunion. Then we could have some fun together. And you could have the money."

"I like the way you kind of ran those together."

"What?"

"Popping into a B and E and then popping over to the reunion. Real fast. You're good at it."

"Don't be cynical, Jack. This is all very straightforward. It's Tuesday and Glen sees patients till ten. He won't be there to bother you."

"I have an obvious question to ask."

"What's that?"

"Why don't you just go get it yourself?"

"Vibes."

"Vibes?"

"The vibes were so bad between us there at the end. If I so much as set a foot back into the place, I'd be depressed for a week. Really."

"Vibes," I said.

She took out five one-hundred-dollar bills and laid them out green and crisp and dignified on the brilliant white tablecloth.

"You'll do it?" she said.

"You really want to get me mixed up in all this?"

"In all what, Jack? It's just getting my suitcase back."

"Why don't you have me do something else?"

"Such as what?"

"Mow your lawn or take out your garbage or something."

"Jack," she said.

And then she put her hand on mine and in a very different way said again, "Jack."

3 The winding asphalt road got steep enough that I had to keep the Toyota in second gear most of the way.

The sun was out now and the hills of pine and spruce were like a wall closing me off from the city behind. At one point I saw a deer come to the edge of the road and watch me with its delicate and frightened beauty.

After a few miles, country-style mailboxes began appearing on the left-hand side of the macadam, and then, up in the trees that seemed to touch the clouds themselves, you could see the sharp jut of the white stone condos, their Frank Lloyd Wright expanse of glass flashing gold in the sunlight.

I rolled down the window and enjoyed the odors, sweet pine and the tang of reasonably fresh water from a nearby creek and wild ginger and ginseng in the forest to the right.

When I saw the box reading GLENDON EVANS, I pulled the Toyota over to the side and parked and got out. At first all I wanted to do was walk a few feet up the asphalt and take in some more of spring's birthing sights, new grass already vivid green and cardinals and blue jays soaring in the air. I looked behind me, at the ragged silhouette of the city in the valley. This was an aerie up here, and Glendon Evans should consider himself damn lucky.

To reach the condo you had to walk eighty-some

stone steps set into a hill at about a sixty-degree angle so narrowly laid out that you could get slapped by overhanging spruce branches all the way up. A squirrel who apparently wanted to get himself adopted accompanied me from a three-foot distance all the way up.

The condo, as imposing as one of the gods of Easter Island, had been set into a piny hill and angled dramatically upward, so that no matter what angle you saw it from, you knew its owner was more powerful than you could ever be. There were three floors. Draperies were drawn on all the windows. The lower level was a two-stall garage. The doors were closed.

Spread across the flagstone patio in front of the place was a variety of lawn furniture, the good doctor apparently getting ready for summer. A redwood picnic table, several lawn chairs, and a gas grill big enough to handle the Bears looked ready for burgers and beer. Only the lonely wind, a bit chill and tart with pine, reminded me that it was still a little early for lawn furniture, and suddenly there was an air of desertion about the place, as if the people who lived here had fled for some mysterious and possibly terrible reason.

I took the key from my pocket again and tried the front door. No problem.

Then I walked into something not unlike a French country house, with raised oak paneling and a limestone fireplace and Persian rugs and built-in bookcases and a leather couch as elegant as a swan's neck. There was a Jim Dine print above the fireplace. The east wall was a fan-shaped window that looked over the winding creek below, still silver with the last of spring's frost. The west wall was a cathedral window from which you could see an impenetrable forest that stretched all the way to a line of ragged hills above which the white tracks of jets now slowly disintegrated against the bright blue sky.

Looking around, I realized that I had made a mistake coming here. Maybe, after twenty-five years of living in places like this, Karen Lane could claim this world as her own, but I couldn't. I was as out of place here as an atheist in a church.

At the last I hadn't even taken her money, just agreed to help her out of some misguided sense that she needed my help. But the condo said very different things to me—that where Karen Lane was concerned, I was the one who needed help, and that it was unlikely that I was here to get anything half as innocent as a suitcase full of "sentimental" things.

I went to the right into a kitchen that kept up the motif of gorgeous capitalistic excess.

Sunlight struck blond wood floors and bleached pine cabinets and a free-standing range that dominated the room. Above the sink, situated to the left of a white wall phone, was an outsize photograph of Karen, done in a mezzotint for dramatic effect. The reverence of the shot told me all I needed to know about the good doctor. He was hooked.

I went back to the living room and was just passing the winding metal staircase where it wound its way to the second level when something splatted on my forehead like a fat warm drop of summer rain.

I reached up and touched a finger to the wet spot on my skin. I brought my finger away and looked at it. There was no doubt at all what it was.

Suddenly I looked around the condo and saw not beautiful furniture of dashing design but all the places somebody with a gun could hide. The afternoon shadows seemed deep now, and I was self-conscious, as if I were being observed.

I took a few steps back and looked up to the second level. Lying even with the border of the carpeted floor was the back of a man's head. He was close to falling off the edge. His dark hair and the shape of his skull were all I could see. There was a bloody knot in the center of his head and it was from this that the blood dropped, tainting the soft gray carpet below.

I took a few deep breaths and wished I had brought my gun and then cursed myself for not bringing my gun and then cursed myself for cursing myself because there had been absolutely no reason I *should* have brought my gun. I'd come here to a psychiatrist's condo to retrieve a suitcase. Not exactly dangerous work.

I went up the winding steps for a closer look at the man.

He wore a monogrammed blue silk dressing robe over a pair of lighter blue cotton pajamas. The monogram read "GE." He wore expensive brown leather house slippers, new enough that you could see the brand name imprinted on the soles. He was maybe six feet and slender and his skin was the color of creamed coffee. But he was one of those black men whose features are as white as Richard Chamberlain's. He was probably my age, but there the similarity ended because he looked brighter and handsomer and, even unconscious, a lot better prepared to put his personal stamp on an impersonal world.

I glanced quickly around the second level. This was an open area with another fan-shaped window to my right and a huge Matisse to the left. You could see dust motes tumble golden in the sunlight. The carpeting was the same light gray as downstairs, and it ran down a long hall with three oak doors on each side.

I lifted up his hand. His pulse was strong. I leaned down and looked closer at his wound. It was open to reveal pink flesh. It would most likely require a few stitches.

I went in search of a bathroom, which proved to be the second door down to the right. On the way I passed a room with a Jacuzzi and a master bedroom laid out to resemble a den where people only occasionally slept.

In the john—or should you call something composed of marble with a sunken bathtub big enough to hold Olympic tryouts a john?—I soaked a towel in warm water and then found some Bactine and Johnson & Johnson Band-Aids and then I filled a paper cup with water about the right temperature to drink.

I was halfway out the bathroom door when I thought about the few times I'd been knocked out back in my police days. I'd forgotten one important thing. I went back to the medicine cabinet, which I noted held any number of brown prescription bottles with Karen Lane's name on them. Among many others, the medicine included Librium and Xanax. Somewhere amid the prescriptions, I found some plain old Tylenol. I thumbed off the lid and knocked three of the white capsules into my hand. When I managed to get him awake, he was going to have a headache and he was going to appreciate these.

I was halfway down the hall, hands loaded with the towel and the Bactine and the Band-Aids and the drinking water and the Tylenol, when he staggered toward me and said, "If you move, I'm going to kill you. Do you understand me?"

"Yes," I said. "Yes, I do understand that."

And I did. He looked to be in pain. He also looked frightened and slightly crazed.

He held in his slender tan hand a fancy silver-plated .45, and I had no doubt at all that he would, for the slightest reason, use it.

"Now," he said, "I want you to lead the way downstairs. We're going to go to the kitchen and sit in the nook and you're going to answer questions, and if you do anything at all that seems suspicious, I'll shoot you right in the belly. All right?"

I hadn't realized till then how badly he was hyperventilating. Nor had I realized that he had begun to sob, his whole torso lunging with cries that seemed half grief and half frenzy.

Then he pitched forward face first and collapsed on the carpet soft and gray as a pigeon's breast.

The gun fell from his hand.

I wondered if I'd underestimated the severity of the head wound.

I wondered if Dr. Glendon Evans hadn't just fallen down dead right in front of my eyes.

4 In one of the kitchen cupboards I found a bottle of Wild Turkey. I poured a lot of it into the coffee I'd made us. Then I carried the cups over to the nook, on the wooden windowsill on which a jay sat, overcome with the soft breeze. Beyond were the hills of pine and the sky of watercolor blue.

"You feeling any better?" I asked him. I sat there and blew on my coffee, having overdone the heat in the microwave, and then I sat about staring at him again.

Twenty-five minutes had passed since I'd helped him downstairs and sat him up on one side of the breakfast-nook table. Twenty-five minutes and he had not uttered a single word. At first I wondered if he wasn't in some kind of shock, but his brown eyes registered all the appropriate emotions to my words, so shock was unlikely. I'd said a few things to irritate him just to see how he would respond, and he'd responded fine. Then I'd considered that maybe he thought I was the man who'd knocked him out, but now he'd know differently. Most burglars didn't put iodine and Band-Aids on the wounds they'd inflicted.

Glendon Evans sat there, a slender, handsome, successful-looking man who even in these circumstances gave off a scent of arrogance. He wasn't talking to me no matter what I said and I didn't know why.

I had some more coffee and then I said, "This is pretty ridiculous. Your not talking, I mean."

He sipped his coffee, set the delicate white china cup back down. Looked out the window.

I said, "Did they want the suitcase?"

This time when he faced me there was more than a hint of anxiety in his eyes.

"So it was the suitcase. You know what was in it?"

He went back to looking out the window. From some distant hill, a red kite had been sent up the air currents where it struggled with comic grace against the soft and invisible tides of spring.

"She told me it had sentimental stuff in it." I paused. "She made it sound very innocent."

I went over and got the bottle and gave us each some more bourbon.

"How's your head?"

He turned and looked and, almost against his will, raised his shoulders in a tiny shrug.

I sat back down and said, "I wonder who's going to get pissed off first. You because you're sick of me talking or me because I'm sick of you not talking."

I congratulated myself on the cleverness of that line, feeling for sure this would open his mouth and get him going magpie-style, but all it produced was a wince and a touch of long fingers to the back of his head.

So I watched the kite for a while, how it angled left, then angled right, red against the light blue sky. It made me recall how warm even March winds were when you were ten and had your hand filled with kite string.

I said, "She did it to you, didn't she?" I knew he wasn't going to talk, so I just kept right on going. "She did it to me when I was twenty. I really thought I was going to marry her and all that stuff. At the time I was working in a supermarket for a dollar thirty-five an hour and spending a dollar twenty-seven on her. I bought myself a forty-nine Ford fastback and one night she gave me a crock about needing it to help her mother and you know what she did? She took a guy to the drive-in in it." My laugh, bitter even after all these years, cracked like a shot in the aerie.

I poured us some more Wild Turkey. His body language—he was leaning forward now and his eyes started studying me—indicated he was getting interested.

He said, "Was that a true story?"

"The drive-in?"

He nodded. He had a great and grave dignity. He certainly had the right demeanor for a shrink.

"True," I said.

Then I went back to staring out the window at the kite and the birds. The silence was back.

I went and found a bathroom and came back. When I slid into my place in the nook I found a new hot cup of coffee in my place. He was pouring Wild Turkey into it.

He said, "Three months ago she told me she desperately needed money for her mother. Some illness. She was very vague. I gave it to her, of course."

"There's something I should tell you."

"You don't need to. I looked through an old scrapbook of hers. Her mother died in nineteen-sixty-four."

"Right."

The pain in his eyes was not simply from the head wound. "I really thought we were going to be married." His lips thinned. "God, what a stupid bastard I was."

"Was she a patient of yours?"

For the first time, he smiled. "A patient? You think she'd ever seek help? Ever think she'd need help? Her version of things is that the world is here to serve her, and if she occasionally has to inconvenience or hurt somebody to be served, then she just hopes there will be no hard feelings. Holly Golightly."

"That's Karen."

"I met her at a party." Miserably, he said, "Her pattern is to have a new one ready to go before she notifies the old one that he's finished."

"You know who the new one is?"

"No. But I'm sure there is one and has been for some time now." His face tightened. "You can tell." He shook his head. "She got calls a few times from a man named Ted Forester. Somehow, I didn't get the impression it was romantic."

So I sat there and thought about Ted Forester and his money and his arrogance. Then I remembered something I hadn't thought about in a quarter century. All the time I'd been going out with Karen, Forester had been skulking in the background, calling her, buying her gifts, waiting me out. She'd admitted this to me one night, saying, "Ted doesn't know what to do with himself now that he's fallen in love with a girl from the Highlands." Which was true enough. It was hard to imagine his parents approving of such a match. Then I spent a moment or two thinking of how Malley and I had smashed out his car window.

Glendon Evans said, "I suppose she told you I hit her."

"No."

"I did. I actually hit her. Not hard. Just sort of a slap. It was something I never thought I could do. Ever."

"She seems to have survived."

"Would you like some more bourbon?"

"No, thanks. Just some more coffee." I was making instant Folgers with tap water and setting it in the microwave. "You want some more?"

"Please."

So I made us some and sat back down and said, "What's in the suitcase?"

"I don't know."

"Really?"

"Really. She kept it in her closet. It had a clasp lock on it. Several times, after things started going badly for us, I was tempted to open it and look inside, but I couldn't see any way to do that without her finding out."

"You never got a glimpse inside?"

"Not a glimpse."

I sipped my coffee. "You have any idea who hit you?"

"None."

"Tell me about it."

He shrugged lean shoulders beneath the expensive blue silk robe. "I came home early today. The flu. I got undressed and into my pajamas and robe and went into the den to lie on the couch and watch the news on cable and that's when somebody came up behind me."

"You remember anything about him?"

"Not really."

"He didn't say anything?"

"No."

"You remember any particular odors or sounds?"

"No."

"How long've you been out?"

"Maybe an hour."

"So he was in here, waiting?"

"Apparently."

"It doesn't sound as if he got the suitcase."

"I know he didn't."

"How do you know?"

"I looked for it yesterday. It was gone."

"You sure she left it behind when she left?"

He touched manicured fingers to his lips. Thought a moment. "That's it. Now I remember. She said she'd pick up the suitcase when Gary Roberts got her things."

"Did she get it then?"

"No. That's the strange thing. He asked for the suitcase, but when I looked for it, it was gone."

"What did Gary say?"

"Oh, he's always polite. He's a holdover from the sixties and he can't let himself consciously admit that it bothers him that she'd live with a black man. He doesn't mean to be a bigot. I feel sorry for him."

"He got all her other things?"

"Yes."

"And he just left without the suitcase?"

"Yes." He thought a moment. "I could be wrong, but I believe the day before Gary came, somebody jimmied one of my windows."

"And got in?"

"Possibly."

Now Karen's coming to me made sense. She had sent Gary over to get her things. When Glendon Evans said the suitcase was gone, she refused to believe him. So she looked me up, sent me in to get it.

"I don't know if I'll ever feel safe here again."

More to myself, I said, "What the hell could be in the suitcase that so many people are interested in it?"

He laughed. "It couldn't be money. Not the way she depended on my Visa and American Express cards." His laugh was as harsh as my own. Then, "The terrible thing is I'd take her back. How about you?"

"Oh, no. She's been out of my system for a long time."

"So why did you agree to help her?"

"We're from the Highlands."

"Oh, yes," he said. "The Highlands."

"So she talked about it?"

"Frequently. She even had nightmares about something that happened back there. Always the same thing. She'd be waking up screaming and bathed in sweat and—" He stared down at his coffee. "My father was a surgeon. I rode around in a Lincoln and went to private school. I almost feel guilty."

I was curious. "She never told you what the nightmares were about?"

"No. But she did always use the same word. Pierce."

"Was that somebody's name?"

"I don't know. I thought you might, being from the Highlands."

"No."

He put a hand to the back of his head. "I'm afraid I'm going to need stitches."

"I was wondering about that."

"Would you give me a ride? There's a trauma center not too far from here."

"Sure."

He stood up. He was still wobbly. He put his palms flat against the table as a precaution.

"You all right?"

He looked up. He looked pale beneath his light-brown skin. I pretended I didn't see the tears in his eyes. "She's never going to come back to me, is she?"

Soft as I could, I said, "I don't think that's her style. Coming back to people, I mean."

5 From a drive-up phone I tried my service to check for calls, discovered I had a radio spot for tomorrow in a downtown studio—a local spot but one that promised decent residuals—and that the same woman had called three times but had not left her name.

Finished with my service, I called Donna Harris' apartment. It was publication time for *Ad World,* and I didn't really expect her to answer—she tended to a bunker mentality the day everything got put to bed, eating innumerable and exotic pieces of junk food (I'd once seen her mix Count Chocula and Trix into a kind of bridge mix)—but she surprised me by being home.

"Hi," she said. "I was hoping you wouldn't call because I'm so damn busy, but then I was hoping you would call because if you didn't, I'd feel neglected. You know?"

"I know."

"I wish we could go to a movie tonight."

"That would be nice, wouldn't it?"

"You finished working?"

"At Security I am. Actually, I'm working on something else."

I explained what that something else was.

Her voice got tight. "You've mentioned her before, haven't you?"

"Karen Lane?"

"Uh-huh."

"Yes, I suppose I have." I sighed. "Please don't do it."

"Do what?"

"Get jealous. There's nothing at all to get jealous about."

"I trust you, Dwyer."

"Really?"

"The rational part of me does, anyway."

"How about the irrational part?"

"How does she look after twenty-five years? God, that sounds like a long time."

"It is a long time, and she doesn't look all that sensational."

"In other words, she looks gorgeous."

"She looks all right."

"Now I know gorgeous for sure."

"It's a job. You seem to forget that little incidental fact. She's actually paying me money."

"Otherwise you probably wouldn't want to get involved with her at all, would you?"

"You probably won't believe this, but no, I wouldn't. She's a classic example of retarded adolescence. Nothing to her matters quite so much as her tan or her new sweater or how that cute guy at the health club looked her over. It's a seventh-grade mentality and we're headed toward fifty. The big five-oh. It's a pain in the ass."

"You figured out what's in the suitcase?"

"Obviously something valuable."

"You think she might have stolen something from somebody?"

It was then I saw it for the first time. The sleek black

Honda motorcycle. Driven by a sleek black-leathered figure. Black leather head to toe, with a black helmet and black mask. Across the street. Just sitting there. I looked back from my rearview and said, "I'm assuming that's what it's all about. Some kind of theft. Otherwise Glendon Evans wouldn't have gotten beaten up."

She sounded a bit scared. "I'm sorry I was so pissy."

"It's all right. You know how I got the other night when that old actor friend of mine stopped by our booth and spent twenty minutes staring at you."

"God, why are we so jealous?"

"Insecure."

"But why are we so insecure? I mean, we're bright, we're attractive. We should have at least a little self-confidence."

"Probably our genes." I looked into the rearview again. The black-clad rider still sat astride his black Honda.

"Your mind is drifting. I can tell over the phone."

"Sorry."

"Something wrong."

"I don't think so. Just my usual paranoia." Then I said, "You could do me a favor."

"What?"

"On your way back to your office, you could stop by my place and pick up some clean clothes for me."

"In other words, you want to stay all night?"

"If you wouldn't mind."

"No, that'd be nice. Only I want the window up."

Donna is never so happy as when she's covered with goose bumps and sleeping soundly. "Can't we flip for it?"

"We flipped for it last time and you cheated."

"Oh, yeah."

"So if you stay, the window's going to be up. Clean fresh air."

"Okay. And I appreciate you stopping by my place. I have the feeling I'm going to be busy."

"Where you going?"

"Up near the Highlands. Little housing development there. Where Karen Lane claims to be staying."

"Claims?"

"Right now, I'm not sure I believe anything she tells me."

"Good." Donna laughed. "Stay that way."

They'd built the houses in the mid-fifties, and though they weren't much bigger than garages, the contractors had been smart enough to paint them in pastels—yellow and lime and pink and puce, the colors of impossible flowers, the colors of high hard national hope—and they were where you strived to live in 1956 if you worked in a factory and wanted the good life as promised by the Democrats and practiced by the Republicans. There were maybe four hundred houses in all, interlocked in Chinese puzzle boxes of streets, thirty to a block, glowing in the sunlight, hickory-smoked with backyard barbecues and driveways filled with installment-plan Ford convertibles and DeSoto sedans. The housing development seemed the quintessence of everything our fathers had fought World War II for. My own father never made it there; we always stayed in the Highlands farther down in the valley. But on Sundays we'd drive in our fifteen-year-old Plymouth with its running boards and mud-flaps through the streets of the development while my parents discussed just which type of house they would buy—there being four basic models—when the money came in.

Now this part of the development was as forgotten as Dwight Eisenhower's golf scores. In the late-afternoon sunlight, the houses looked faded now, and scraped in places and smashed in others, tape running the length of some picture windows, and chain-link fences giving some of the tiny homes the air of fortresses, particularly those with Day-Glo BEWARE OF DOG signs. Blacks and Chicanos were pushing up the valley now, taking the same route as these whites had twenty-five years earlier. But you saw a lot of Dixie-flag decals on the bumper stickers of the scrap-heap cars along the curb, and you saw in the eyes of the ten- and eleven-year-old kids—already wheezing on cigarettes and walking with their arms possessively around girls every bit as tough as the boys—you saw the sum total of decades of hatred. Meals, at least steady ones, were something you had to fight for up here, and blacks, to feed their own families, meant by one way or another to take your meals. So you had the old lady sew an NRA decal on your work jacket, and you even—just for curiosity's sake—went to the Klan rally held out on an outlying farm. You wouldn't kill a black man personally, but you wouldn't condemn someone who had.

The Roberts home was freshly painted white, and a new white Chevrolet sedan sat in the drive. The place was so clean and neat, it must have made its neighbors want to come over and smear dirt on it out of sheer envy.

I parked behind the Chevrolet and got out. A collie came up. He was bathed and smelled clean when he put his front paws on my stomach and asked to be petted. From this angle I could see into the backyard. There was a clothesline filled with white sheets and shirts and the kind of pink rayon uniform waitresses wear. Beneath the sheets flapping like schooner masts in the breeze, I saw a pair of jean-clad legs.

I went back to the clothesline, the collie keeping me eager and friendly company, and when I got there I said, "Susan?"

And then I saw the feet go up on tippy-toes and saw her head appear over the sheets.

"My God," she said.

She was older now but still pretty. There was only a little gray in the otherwise auburn hair, and as she came around the sheets, I saw that she'd put on just a few pounds—far fewer than I had—and looked trim in her white blouse and blue man's cardigan and pleasantly snug jeans. In high school she'd always been one of my favorite people—she'd had a kind of wisdom that I attributed to the early loss of her father; she knew what mattered and what did not—and just the way her brown eyes watched me now, with humor and curiosity, I knew she was still going to be one of my favorite people.

"I don't believe it," she said. Then she smiled. "It's really nice seeing you."

"It's really nice seeing you." I nodded to the clothes, the pink waitress uniform, the shirts, the sheets. "I didn't know people still hung wash out."

She laughed. "I do because it's the cleanest smell in the world. Here. Grab one of those sheets and smell it."

"You serious?"

"Of course I'm serious."

So I did and it smelled wonderful, clean as she'd promised.

"I see you on TV. On commercials. You're a good actor."

"I'm learning."

"It must be exciting."

"Sometimes." I nodded to the house. "How's Gary?"

For the first time, her face tightened. "He's in there working."

"He sell anything yet?"

"Stories here and there."

38

"He'll make it. You can't lose faith."

"That's the funny thing. I haven't, but he has." She shook her head. "He's been writing stories since we were in high school, right? That's why he went into teaching high school English, so he could stay close to what he loved. Well, he finally got some real interest on a novel a few weeks ago—after nearly twenty years of trying—and he burns it."

"He burned the novel?"

"Yes. Said it wasn't good enough."

She shrugged, glanced down at her hands. She had always been pretty rather than beautiful, with an almost mournful grace. It was a grace that had only deepened as she got older. Then she smiled and I wanted to hold her, she gave me that much sense of tenderness. "I'll bet I know why you're here."

"She here?"

"No. But she called. Said she'd see us at the reunion dance tonight. You going?"

"I hadn't planned on it. But if it's the only way I can see her, I will."

She said, "You're not starting up with her again, are you?"

"Do I look crazy?"

"I shouldn't have said that. She's my friend."

"She can still be your friend and you can still tell the truth."

"She's pretty messed up. All those husbands." She reached out and took an edge of the sheet and brought it to her nose. "I always associate this smell with my mother. I always helped her hang out the wash and I loved to put my face against wet clothes and let them freeze my cheeks till my skin got numb." She inhaled the aroma. "Unfortunately, I can't convince either of my kids to help me. It's a different age." She put the sheet back down. "But I was talking about Karen, wasn't I? She's kind of a basket case."

"She also may be in some serious trouble."

"Why?"

I started to tell her, but then the back door opened and a small, slight man with thinning brown hair caught back in a ponytail and rimless eyeglasses came up. Gary.

"God," he said and put out his slender hand. We shook. He looked much older than Susan, and much wearier. He was still thin, but it was a beaten thin, and his clothes were redolent of the sixties, faded tie-dye shirt and bell-bottoms, like a hobo looking for the ghost of Jim Morrison. Gary and I had lived two blocks away from each other in the Highlands, and sometimes I'd gone to his parents' apartment, where we smoked Luckies and drank Pepsis all afternoon and listened to Elvis and Carl Perkins and Little Richard, dreaming of owning custom cars and having as our own the women Robert Mitchum always ended up with. But that was just one side of Gary.. He'd had a battered bookcase filled with paperbacks reverently filed alphabetically, everything from Arthur C. Clarke to John O'Hara, from Allen Ginsburg to e.e. cummings (he'd gotten me into Jack Kerouac, an affection I've never lost), and the only time I'd ever seen him hit somebody was one afternoon when a kid drunk on 3.2 beer tripped into Gary's bookcase, knocking a brand-new Peter Rabe to the floor. Gary, not big, not known for his temper, slapped the kid across the face with the precision of a fabled pachuco opening up somebody's gullet with a shiv. Now we stood on either side of twenty-five years and he said, "God, look at you."

"Look at you."

"I mean, you look great, Jack. I look like a sixty-year-old man."

And I heard then what had always been in him—some generalized bitterness, half self-pity, half frustration with a world that had passed your old man by and was intent on doing the same thing to you—and I glanced over at Susan, who watched her husband with the same concern she'd always had for him. In ninth grade she'd simply adopted him in some curious way, part maternal and part sexual, and she had never let go of that impulse or of him down all these long years.

Gary said, "We see you on TV."

"Yeah." Then, "How about letting me read some of your stories?"

"Oh, they're not much. You know that."

"Really, I'd like to read some." And I wanted to, too. He had the early knack for telling stories, very good ones when he wrote in the vein of the magazines we both liked, *Manhunt* and *Ellery Queen,* less so when he affected the styles he found in the *New Yorker* and the *Atlantic.*

"Hubris," he said.

"Why?"

Gently, she said, "He wrote a perfectly good detective story three months ago but wouldn't send it off."

"Why not send it out?"

"I don't want to be a detective writer. I want to be a real writer."

And then I remembered how he'd shifted somewhere in college, telling me about it one night behind a couple of joints and some wine, how popular fiction had started to bore him, how it was "genius" or nothing. So now he had a tract home and graying hair in a ponytail and he took the efforts of his heart and mind and burned them. Much as I liked him, and felt sentimental watching him now, he seemed alien to me somehow, aggrieved in a way that he wanted to be literary but which came off as merely pathological.

41

One of those awkward silences fell between us, until Susan said, "Jack thinks Karen's in some trouble."

His head snapped up. His blue eyes looked agitated behind his rimless glasses. "What kind of trouble?"

"I'm not sure," I said. "Something to do with a missing suitcase. Do you know anything about it?"

"Nothing about a suitcase," Susan said.

"Gary?"

"No. Nothing." But his air of anxiety continued. He reminded me of how Glendon Evans had acted earlier that afternoon.

"Kids," Susan said.

"What?"

"That's her trouble. No children."

Gary said, "That isn't her trouble."

"No?" I asked.

"No. Her trouble is that people think she's one thing when she's another."

"What is she, then?"

He flushed, seeing how seriously I'd taken his statement. Then he put on a big party smile. "You shouldn't pay any attention to a forty-two-year-old man who's gotten more than two hundred rejections in his time."

I wasn't going to let him go so easily—I wanted to press him on his remark—but Susan said, "I'm afraid you drove out here for nothing."

"Not for nothing. I got to see you."

"You should take a few pointers from Jack, Gary."

He put out his hand again. "Well, I'm going to try to squeeze in a few more pages before dinner. Hope you'll excuse me."

"I really would like to see some of your work."

"Sure, Jack." Then he sort of cuffed me on the arm and left.

We watched him go inside. When he was gone, Susan said, "He has a surprise coming.

"What?"

"The detective story he thought he burned. He set it on fire in the fireplace, but I got most of it out. It's only singed."

"You've read it?"

"Not yet. But I know it'll be good. I'll send it in even if he doesn't want me to. Am I being a bitch?"

I laughed. "Somehow, Susan, I can't imagine you ever being a bitch."

"You always idealized me."

"I guess it's your eyes and your hands. They were always exceptional."

"Well, I can't tell you how nice it is to hear things like that. If I didn't have to go get dinner, I'd ask you to keep right on talking."

I said, "So you don't know anything about a suitcase?"

"No. She's never mentioned anything."

"And nobody's tried to break into your place?"

She said, "My God, no. Now you've really got me scared."

"I'd just keep everything locked up, tight."

She looked a bit older now, her brow tense with worry. "What's going on, Jack?"

"I don't know."

"She really is in trouble, isn't she?"

"Yes. But as usual, she only gives you half the facts, so you can't be sure what's going on."

"She's my friend, as I said, but she can be a very frustrating woman."

"Yeah, I seem to remember that."

"I felt so bad for you. You know, the way she treated you back then."

I smiled. "I appreciate that—but it was probably a good experience for me. Taught me about things."

"You know, I've never believed that. I think a part of

you should stay naive and unhurt all your life. I've never understood why pain is supposed to be good for you."

I laughed. "Now that you mention it, neither do I. But you've been lucky. You've always had Gary, and he's always had you."

"I'm sure we've both been tempted. Even up here among all the unfashionable Highlands people—" saying this with just the slightest sardonic touch— "adultery is the favorite. Until AIDS came along, most of my best friends were always having affairs while their husbands were at the factories. But there was so much pain—" She shook her head. "I suppose it's exciting—"

"Take my word for it, you haven't missed anything."

"Somehow I believe you."

She'd picked up the sheet again, smelled it. Dusk was a gauzy haze in which you could hear the suppertime laughter of children and the stern voices of TV anchormen enumerating the terrors of the day. Setting the sheet back, she said, "I'm glad you finally found some excuse to come up here."

"Yeah, me, too."

"I always liked you. Is that okay to say?"

"That's wonderful to say."

Then the pain was back in her eyes. "We were going to the reunion tonight, but Gary backed out. The last few months . . ." She shook her head. "Maybe you could take him out for some beer some night. Cheer him up. I can't seem to do it."

"I'd like that," I said, and I would, though I knew I'd never do it. "I'd like that very much."

She stared at me then. "You've been lucky."

"Pretty much."

"You got out of the Highlands."

"It's not so bad."

"You know better." She frowned. "He should've let me work. I could've helped us find a house somewhere else. Living here—it does something to you. You know how it is here, Jack. I just keep thinking maybe he would really have turned out to be a writer if we hadn't lived here. You know?"

I kissed her on the cheek, caught the scent of the clean wash again, and left. "Maybe he'll be a writer yet."

She smiled. "You know what his problem is?"

"What?"

"He isn't a boy anymore."

"He's nearly forty-three. He shouldn't be a boy."

"But he should still have some fun. He never has any fun. He just writes stories and tears them up and says they're not good enough."

I let her lean into me and we stood a moment, the air fresh with her laundry and the smell of new grass, and hamburgers grilling on the back porch next door.

"Can you believe we're twenty-five years older?" she said. "Sometimes it's scary, isn't it?"

"That's the right word for it, Susan. Scary."

I hugged her and listened for a time to the children in the dusk, their laughter like pure water, and then I went and got into my car and started back through the maze of streets. I had one other person I wanted to talk to about Karen, somebody I was not looking forward to seeing at all.

I was halfway there when I happened to glance in my rearview and found that not all my paranoia is unjustified.

Somebody in black leather on a black Honda cycle was accompanying me.

6 The Highlands has a shopping district of four blocks, stores that even back in the forties looked old, two-story brick jobs mostly, with the names of their original owners carved in fancy cursive somewhere near the roof, the names running to Czech and Irish, with the polysyllables of an occasional Italian name also being included. Growing up, I'd come here with my parents to shop for groceries or to buy something from the hardware store or the auto-parts store or to get a shirt from the secondhand store (when you really had dough you went to Penney's), but shopping centers had killed all that off now—you drove out to one of five malls on this side of town that had taken the place of the merchants who had settled and helped build this area since as far back as 1849, when six thousand people migrated up here from the Virginias. Now you didn't have merchants, you had tavern-owners. That's all that was left now, bars advertising naked women and country-Western music and big-screen Bears games, with a store that sold fancy cowboy clothes or a concrete lot filled with the sad hulks of used cars thrown in to serve the workingmen who bring their paychecks and their beaten hopes down here. When you come here at night, it's not so bad, with workers from the slaughterhouse a mile away and their Czech girlfriends wandering from tavern to tavern like people out of a John Steinbeck novel. But in the daylight you see how everything needs paint and how the walks are cracked, and you see all the names spray-painted on the sides of the taverns, lurid reds and blacks and green on whitewashed surfaces; KILL QUEERS! NIGGERS SUCK! MEXES STAY OUT!

I pulled my car into the half-empty lot of a place called The Nook (needless to say, regulars called it The Nookie), and walked behind a couple of men with black lunch pails through the front door, smelling the silty residue from the hog kill. The air smells and feels a certain way when cows are killed. Hog kills fill the air with textures and odors all their own.

The interior, long bar on the left wall, three bumper pool tables down the center, booths and pinball games to the left, got rid of the hog odor anyway, replacing it with beer, cigarette smoke, microwave pizza, sweat, and perfume. The perpetually turning BUDWEISER sign hanging over the cash register and the wide space-age-model Seeburg jukebox (drop in two quarters and it would take you to Pluto, and play you a couple of Hank Williams, Jr., tunes along the way) and the pinball games with their busty ladies and the discreet little red plastic electric candles in the booths gave the long, low, dark place most of its light. The mood was jovial now—the men buying paycheck rounds of shots-and-beer and the women treated with outsize courtesy—but by nine it would all change and there would be at least a few fistfights, savage ones. Back in my police days, I'd come into dozens of places like this one and seen enough blood to rival the killing floor where many of these men worked—eyes hooked out with thumbs, throats ripped open with broken beer bottles, noses smashed in with working-shoe heels, and women slapped so hard and so long that their faces were swollen beyond recognition. But it was the women who were the most curious of all, because when you tried to arrest the husbands or boyfriends who'd done this to them, the women would jump on you, physically try to stop you from dragging their men to the curb and the car. It was as if they understood how miserable the lives of their men were and therefore forgave them nearly any atrocity.

I ordered a shell and had some beer nuts and looked around to see if I could see Chuck Lane, and when I didn't see him said to the bartender, whose arms were so thick with tattoos they looked like some kind of shimmering snakeskin, "You seen Chuck?"

"So who wants to know?"

"Friend of his sister's."

He shot me a smirk. "His sister's got a lot of friends." He put a fat left finger to his right nostril and snuffled like a cokehead in need. He was short and meaty with sideburns of a length and width I hadn't seen since 1967. His teeth were dirty little stubs. He had a blue gaze that combined malice and stupidity with chilling ease. If Richard Speck had a brother, this guy was it. "Rich ones, too, from what I hear. And you don't look like no rich one."

I sighed. "I just want to see Chuck. It's important. So if he's here, I'd appreciate it if you'd let him know that Jack Dwyer wants to talk to him."

"It worth five to you?"

"That's only in movies. Just call Chuck."

"I need some grease to do it because I got to walk all the way down the basement stairs. The intercom's on the blink."

"Consider it good exercise."

"I got an inflamed prostate. It hurts to walk."

"Goddamn, are you serious? You're going to make me pay you five bucks to go get Chuck?"

"Yeah."

"Why don't I just go down there myself?"

"He won't let you in unless you know the password.

He's got, you know, bill collectors and like that after him."

"So I have to give you five bucks to go get him?"

"I ain't kiddin' you about the prostate." And with that he produced a brown prescription bottle and rattled it at me like some voodoo icon. "This is a legit prescription right from the doc." He kind of grabbed his crotch and frowned. "It's like I got this baseball between my legs and it's real hard to move."

So I laid five on the bar.

"Tell you what. While you're waitin', you have another shell and it'll be on Kenny."

"Who's Kenny?"

"Me."

"Oh, yeah. Thanks."

So Kenny, whose very theatrical walk reminded me of Charles Laughton as the Hunchback of Notre Dame, asked a biker-like guy two stools down from mine, "You watch the register for me, Mike?"

"Anybody touches that sumbitch," Mike said, showing a gloved fist the size of a baseball mitt, "he's dead meat."

I had to make sure to bring Donna here next time we kind of wanted to relax and enjoy a quiet evening.

"So you're looking for Karen."

"Right."

"Mind if I ask why?"

"Yeah, I do mind."

He shook his head. "You still don't like me, do you, Dwyer?"

I sighed. "It doesn't matter, Chuck."

"You think because I live down here, I don't have any pride?"

I looked around. His "apartment" was one big room with imitation knotty pine walls and the sort of furniture you find at garage sales. There was an aged Ziv black-and-white TV with enough aluminum foil on the rabbit ears to cook several steaks in. There was a multi-colored throw rug, meant to resemble a hooked rug, and you could see stiff patches where somebody had spilled things or thrown up.

This was about where you would expect to find Chuck Lane twenty-five years later. "Luckless" was the word for him. He'd been born with a clubfoot, and when he walked the movement was so violent and awk-ward, you forgave him any sin because you could gauge the physical pain and humiliation he felt just try-ing to get down the street. But there was a lot to for-give him for. He was a thief—in eighth grade, he'd taken my baseball glove, and I had yet to forget it—and he'd always played on the fringes of real crime, doing favors for punks who enjoyed brief power with hot-car rings or shoplifting rings or by hiring out to smash up people who owed money or who were plug-ging their private parts into places they didn't belong. In the early sixties Chuck had distinguished himself by trying to give his girlfriend an abortion in the back seat of his car with a coat hanger and a great deal of stu-pidity. She'd bled to death all over the seat covers and the floor, Chuck frozen in fear that he'd go to the slammer for murder. He didn't. He went to the slam-mer for manslaughter. When he got out, he came to work here at the tavern, which was owned by another man who lived on the periphery of law. But by this time in his life, Chuck wasn't more than a part-time bartender and occasional petty thief. He played a lot of poker. He wasn't any better at it than he was at any-thing else. During the days I'd gone out with Karen, I'd learned how much she'd loved him but also how much of a burden he was, always in need of money or a place to hide or, simply, comfort, his mental stability never having been the best.

Now he was in his forties and heavyset and shaggy with a reddish beard and the kind of colorful Saturday-night clothes that had gone out with leisure suits.

"Why're you looking for Karen?"

I sighed. "Chuck, I'm asking you a straightforward question. Do you know where Karen is?" I wanted to see her for a simple reason. To tell her how Glendon Evans was knocked unconscious, to get a simple, honest answer as to what was really in the suitcase.

"I ain't seen her."

"Right."

"I'm telling you the truth."

He got up from his overstuffed chair and crossed the room to get at a carton of Camels. I had to look away. I'd always felt ashamed of myself around him, ashamed, I guess, that my limbs were intact. He didn't deserve to be born crippled. Nobody did.

He tore open a new pack and said, "She in some kind of trouble or something?"

"You know anything about a suitcase?"

His sister's eyes stared at me. "Suitcase?"

"Right."

"Uh-uh."

He moved across the floor again. I looked away. "Still embarrasses you, don't it?"

"What?"

"My foot."

I didn't say anything.

"You always was that way, Dwyer." He laughed then and I didn't know why he laughed; all I knew was that he'd just shown me teeth badly in need of a dentist.

I wanted out of there, then. The mildew smell, the beer smell, the sagging single bed, the shabby clothes. I wondered what he dreamed of, what could possibly keep him going in these circumstances. There was not even a window to look out of. Only a few years ago he'd been a teenager, when there was always the hope that the cards would run good, but the cards hadn't run good at all for him.

"How about this suitcase?" he said.

"What about it?"

"What's in it?"

"I'm not sure."

"Why you want it?"

"Because I was hired to find it."

"But you don't know what's in it?"

"That's right, Chuck. I don't know what's in it."

He smiled.

"What's funny?"

"It's Karen, isn't it?"

"Karen?"

"Sure. This sounds like some kind of deal she'd get you involved in. Having you look for something but not telling you what it is exactly."

I glanced around. He had a poster of Farrah Fawcett in a swimsuit and a RE-ELECT REAGAN bumper sticker on the wall. Sitting on a bureau was a travel brochure to sunny Arizona with an envelope that looked to contain an airline ticket. "You ever think of moving out of this place?"

"It getting to you?"

"Sort of, I guess."

"Gets to me, too." He shrugged. "It's about all I can afford these days. After the Amway thing went to shit, I mean."

"You sold Amway?"

"Yeah. You ever go to any of their meetings?"

"Uh-uh."

"Man, they get you all het up. It's like going to one

of them TV evangelists. One night I was watchin' the tube here and I was pretty gassed up on beer and this TV evangelist came on and I watched him, really watched him for the first time, and I'll be damned if I didn't stand up and pledge myself to Jesus, and I mean I had tears streamin' down my cheeks, and I wrote him out a check for one hundred dollars and staggered down to the post office and mailed it in. It was like this light was shining in my eyes, this real strong light, and for about an hour or so it was like I was on this high I'd never been on before, really whacked out, you know, better than drugs or sex or booze or anything." Then he stopped and sighed. "But then in the morning I got up and remembered what I'd done, sending the check in and all, and I remembered that I'd closed that account and that the check would bounce and—" He smoked some of his cigarette. "Anyway, Amway was like that for a while. I'd go to these meetings and get real psyched up, but then . . ."

He let it drift off, the way so much in his life had drifted off.

The room was getting oppressive again.

"She's getting it together."

"Karen?" I said.

"Yeah. She dumped that spook."

Which almost caused me to smile, never understanding why one set of outcasts wants to put down another set of outcasts. Didn't he see that the same people who dismissed him as a clubfoot probably dismissed Glendon Evans for being black?

"But you don't know where she is?"

"Not really, man. She calls sometimes. I'll tell her you're looking for her."

"So you don't know anything about a suitcase?"

"Why you keep asking? I already said no. Jesus,

man." He stubbed out his cigarette. "It's because of the baseball glove, isn't it?"

"Nah."

"Bullshit."

"Well."

"I take a crummy baseball glove thirty years ago and you still blame me."

I felt myself flush.

"People change, you know, Dwyer."

"I know." He had me feeling guilty. He had me feeling the way he wanted me to feel.

"I don't know from no suitcase, all right?"

"All right."

"And the next time you come down here, try not to look like you just walked into a leper colony, all right? Like you're going to get contaminated or something?"

I stood up. Held out my hand. "Good to see you, Chuck."

He got up and getting up was an effort and I averted my eyes and he saw me avert my eyes and then he shook my hand and said, "Being a gimp isn't so bad, Dwyer. It's other people *thinking* it's so bad that really gets to you, you know?"

I babbled. "Take it easy, Chuck."

"Right. That's how I always take it. Easy. I've got the charmed life, you know."

7 These days they have names like The Dead Kennedys and The Sea Hags and The Virgin Prunes, and when my sixteen-year-old son plays them for me I try to remember that back in my sixteen-year-old days I drove my own parents crazy with some very offensive people named Little Richard and Howlin' Wolf and, not least, Elvis himself.

Now I stood outside a four-story brick building in the middle of the Highlands looking up at a sky filled with stars and a slice of quarter moon and tumbling clouds the color of ghosts. There was no sign of a black Honda.

From inside St. Michael's came a medley of songs, including "Don't Be Cruel" and "Sea of Love" and "Blue Jean Bop" and "Runaround Sue" and "Walkin' to New Orleans," all done with feverish amateurish fun. I wanted for the sake of my son to enjoy the music of The Dead Kennedys, but maybe it was my age or the calculated offensiveness of their name, but when he showed me their album cover I had an instant fantasy about putting them up against a wall and punching their faces in. I didn't say that to my son, of course. I just put my arm around him and said, "Whatever happened to that Dion and the Belmonts tape I gave you?"

"It was all right till I found out what he's doing these days."

"What's that?"

"Making religious albums."

"Really?"

"Yeah, Dad, and I just have a real hard time taking anybody seriously who makes religious albums. Like all those ministers on cable. You know?"

So Dion, once of rock 'n' roll leather and rock 'n' roll heat, was making a very different kind of album now and maybe even believing the too-sweet, too-easy hype of commercial religion, and who the hell was I to judge him anyway? And now here I was standing outside the school where nearly forty years ago I'd started kindergarten and where twenty-five years ago I'd graduated high school. I had a Bud in one hand and a cigarette in another (these days I don't smoke more than ten cigarettes a week, just enough to keep myself worried and guilty and coughing), and I heard music that should have lifted me back to other times when you measured success by the kind of car you drove or whom you hung out with or what base (first, second, or third) you'd gotten to the night before. But all I sensed now was how time cheated you, tricked you, and one day you were young and then one day you were not young. And then people you loved began dying so that one funeral service became very much like another, the grimace on the faces of those bearing the casket, the chill silver drops of holy water sprinkled on the newly turned earth, the sound of tears lost in the cold wind and the flapping sound of the canvas tent at graveside. And so you stood on nights like this, the stars washed across the endless sky, and just tried to make simple animal sense of it all. But you couldn't, of course, because ultimately it made sense to none of us, not the priest who whispered solace nor the hedonist who tried to deny it in the noisy illusion of his passion nor the puzzled six-year-old trapped in the confines of a white hospital bed he'd never leave. All you could understand was how many millions had stood on just such evenings down the time-stream thinking the same thoughts and coming to the same conclusion, which was really no conclusion at all, just the hope, even among the most cynical of men, that there really was a God or something very much like a God, and that all this did indeed have significance somehow in the relentless cosmic darkness.

"Say, there's a Shamrock!" cried a drunken male voice.

And like some berserk chorus line, three people came down the front steps of the school, doing some kicks and singing along to "Take Good Care of My Baby."

"He *is* a Shamrock!" cried both of the women on either side of the chubby man. He was bald and plump and wore a red dinner jacket and a cummerbund wide as a pillowcase and a wonderful boozy grin. The women were also plump and wore clever gowns that disguised their widening middles and pushed up voluptuously their fortyish cleavage. The way they did their kicks and sang the tune aloud, they were like an Ample Lady version of the Rockettes and they were exactly what I needed to pull me out of my hole.

"Yeah, I'm a Shamrock," I said, the word on my tongue as silly as it'd ever been. The public schools had always had names like Wilson Wolverines and Roosevelt Rough Riders. We'd gotten stuck with Shamrocks. I'd just always known that Bogart would never have let anybody call him a Shamrock. Not without hitting the guy, anyway.

"Take it from me," the drunk said, "spike your own punch. It's too weak otherwise."

"Georgie has his own bottle," explained one of the women in a loud proud voice.

The other woman giggled. "He also has his own wife. But we lost her a while back."

So they staggered on to the car and I went inside and the first thing I noticed was that they still used the same kind of floor wax they had for the past uncountable decades, the smell of it making me feel like I was imprisoned in a time capsule: a ten-year-old on an autumn day sitting in a desk at the back ostensibly reading my history book with a Ray Bradbury paperback carefully tucked inside.

"Jack Dwyer."

She sat at one of the two long tables where you checked in and got your name tag.

I had to glimpse at hers quickly so I'd remember who she was. "Hi, Kathy." Kathy Malloy.

"You didn't answer our RSVP. We didn't expect you. Looks like you might have made up your mind at the last minute." She tried to put a laugh on the line but it didn't work. The way her eyes scanned my rumpled tweed jacket and white tieless button-down shirt and Levi's and five-o'clock shadow, I could see that she hadn't changed any. She was one of those people born to be a hall monitor, to watch very closely what you did and to disapprove the hell out of it. She had gray hair now, worn in one of those frothing things that seem to be white women's version of an Afro, and she wore a red silk dress that despite its festive color was redolent of nothing so much as blood. She said, "Helen Manner is supposed to be helping out at the table here." She leaned forward. "Between you and me, I think Helen's developed a drinking problem over the years. She runs inside to the punch bowl every chance she gets. Don't say anything to anybody, though, all right?"

Kathy Malloy had probably done everything but rent a sound truck to broadcast Helen Manner's drinking problem and here she was telling me not to tell anybody. Right.

I got through the rest of it as quickly as I could, signing some things, accepting my name tag, hearing some more gossip, and then I went into the gym, which was like a vast dark cave festooned with low-hanging crepe of green and white, with a stage at front prowled by chunky guys my own age in gold-lamé outfits who, despite their lack of talent, seemed to be having one hell of a good time. Above the stage was a banner that said WELCOME CLASS OF '63, and I realized then how '63 looked as ancient as '23 or '17. I recalled a time when I couldn't believe it was ever going to be 1970. Now we were facing down the gun barrel of 1990. What was going on here?

For the first twenty minutes, I mingled. I was looking for Karen Lane and not finding her and in the process I renewed a lot of acquaintances, some reluctantly, some gladly, learning all those things that somehow measure lifetimes these days—the one who was married three times, the one who was wealthy at least with money, the one who was battling cancer, the one who had turned out gay, the skinny one who had turned fat or the fat one who was now a beauty, the one who was a florid-faced alcoholic, the one who was the cuckold, the one who was the menopausal male with the woman half his age. The ones you'd envied and wished in your petty heart the worst for—they'd all seemed to do pretty well, Buick-comfortable and suburban-smug. And the ones you'd feared for—the ones with limps and lisps and those little spasms of intolerable anxiety or even madness—they stood now in a cluster of the twisted and forsaken, accepting the smiles and salutations of their betters with the same kind of sad gratitude they'd long ago gotten used to.

And I still didn't see Karen Lane, though, according to various people I asked, I was drawing close—she'd just been seen on the dance floor, or at the bar, or out the back door, where a few people stood by the garage where the monsignor had parked his infamous black '57 Dodge (the primo fantasy of the time having been making out with your girl in its back seat). Joints and wine were being passed around among people who seemed almost fanatical in their laughter and who seemed to remember details of twenty-five years ago that I'd forgotten entirely.

I asked a man I recognized as a lawyer if he'd seen Karen Lane. He said, "Seen her? Hell, man, she's so gorgeous, I fell in love with her." Then he nodded to the alley behind. "I think she went out there with Larry Price."

I stood there and stared at him and time was a trap of spiderwebbing I couldn't escape. Even after a quarter century, her being with Larry Price had the power to enrage me.

I pushed past the partiers and on out to the alley where a block-long of sagging garages, probably new about the time Henry Ford was rolling his first Model T off the assembly line, stood like wooden gravestones in the moonlight. They smelled of old wood and car oil and moist earth.

I looked up and down the long shadows and saw nothing. I was about to turn around and go back to the party when I heard the unmistakable moan.

Two garages away.

My stomach became fiery with pain and I felt the blind, unreasoning impulse of jealousy.

I wanted to turn around and go back to the school, and as I started to move toward the monsignor's garage again, I heard the slap, sharp as a gunshot.

Then in the soft night I heard Karen say, "Leave, Larry. Please."

"I'm not finished."

"But I'm finished, Larry, and I have been for a long time."

"I'm sick of that goddamn tale of yours, Karen. You know that? It goddamn happened and it's goddamn over and nothing can goddamn be done about it."

"Please, Larry."

"Bitch."

Then he slapped her. A clean slap, probably more harmful emotionally than physically. "Bitch."

He came out of one of the garages down in the shadows and looked around as if an assassin might be waiting for him. He had changed very little—six feet, blond, attentive to his tan and his teeth. He sold BMWs and Volvos, mostly during long lunches at the Reynolds Country Club.

He was drunk enough that he leaned perilously forward as he moved. He almost bumped into me before he saw me.

"Hey—"

And I dropped him. For a variety of reasons, only one even remotely noble—because he'd slapped her. The second was because he'd beaten me in high school, and the third because I was frustrated with the lies Karen had been telling me and I'd had just enough vodka-laced punch to work up a mean floating edge.

"God," he said, feeling his jaw and shaking his head.

By now, she was out in the moon shadows, staring down at him. "What happened?"

"He slapped you, didn't he?"

She glanced sharply at me. "What are you doing here, Jack?"

"Looking for you."

"Did you get the suitcase?"

"We need to talk about that, Karen. We need to talk very long and very hard about that."

If she hadn't screamed, I might not have seen him lunge at me.

I got him a hard clean shot in the stomach and then clubbed his temple with the side of my fist. He dropped to his knees and started vomiting.

"I can't watch this," she said, starting to pace in hysterical little circles. In her blue jersey jumper and white beads, she resembled a society woman who has just been informed that the entire family fortune has been embezzled.

Then, gathering herself, she went over to him and said, "Are you all right, Larry?"

"What the hell you doing with him?"

"He's helping me find something."

"What?"

"It needn't concern you." She sounded as prim as a schoolmarm. "I merely asked if you were all right."

But now he didn't pay any attention to her. He struggled to his feet, leaning back a bit from the booze. He was more sober now. Losing some blood and throwing up can occasionally work wonders.

"You think you're going to get away with this, Dwyer, you're really crazy. Really crazy." Then he turned on her and said, "You too, bitch. You too."

He left.

He walked bowlegged the way Oliver Hardy had in *Way Out West*. He wanted to walk mean because he was a basically mean guy and booze only enhanced his anger. But right now all he could do was look like Oliver Hardy and it didn't scare me and it didn't impress me and I'd already decided that if he came back, I was going to put a few more fists into him.

"That wasn't necessary."

"Sure it was," I said.

"You don't understand the situation here."

"I understand that Larry Price is a jerk and always has been."

"But that's all you understand."

"I met Dr. Evans."

Her eyes narrowed. "He was there when you went into the apartment?"

"He was there all right. Unconscious."

"What?"

"And bleeding."

She sighed. Shook her head. "So he did try it."

"Try what?"

"Suicide."

"Sorry."

"What?"

"Somebody hit him across the back of the head. Very hard. And several times. Guess what they were looking for."

"His money, probably. Some junkie or something."

"God, you're just going to keep it up, aren't you?"

"Keep what up? What are you talking about?"

"Keep up this guise that there's something very innocent in the suitcase and that you just kind of want it back for old times' sake. Are you dealing drugs?"

"My God, what kind of person do you think I am?"

"Did you do some jewelry salesman out of his ruby collection?"

"I don't want to hear any more."

"Somebody wants whatever's in that suitcase badly enough to risk B and E and assault with a deadly weapon. Those are heavy raps." I grabbed her by the shoulder—thinking that Glendon Evans had told me he'd hit her—and I dug my thumb and forefinger into her gentle and wonderful flesh. "You owe it to me, Karen."

"What?"

"The truth."

She laughed without seeming at all amused. "Oh, I wish I knew the truth, Jack. How I wish I knew the truth."

But I was in no mood for philosophy. "What's in the suitcase?"

"Would you make me a promise?"

"What?"

"If we went back into the gym and danced the slow dance medley, would you promise not to step on my feet?"

"Don't try to buy me off, Karen. I want to know what the hell's going on. You're in trouble, whether you know it or not."

"You used to be a terrible dancer, Jack, and for some reason I suspect you still are." She leaned up and kissed my cheek and I felt blessed and cursed at the same time. "But then you're cute and you're sincere, and sometimes those things are even more important than the social graces."

"Have you always been this superficial?"

"No," she said, and there was an almost startling melancholy in her voice. "No, Jack, I've had to work at it. I really have."

Then she took my arm and led me back inside the gym where in tenth grade she'd given me a lingering public kiss right there on the dance floor. Robert Mitchum had nothing on me.

So we started dancing, a little formally at first, as the band went through some Connie Francis numbers and then some Johnny Mathis numbers and then some Teddy Bear numbers, and I started looking around the shadows of the gym at the joke being played out before me.

Here were the kids I'd made my First Communion with and played baseball with and walked home from school with along the railroad tracks that smelled of grease and swapped comics with (Batman was always worth two of anything else) and watched change from little girls into big girls with powers both wonderful and terrible over me and little boys into half-men with a hatred that could only come from growing up in the Highlands—but whatever else we'd been, we'd been young and it had all been ahead of us—the great promise of money and achievement and sex, God yes, sex. But these people were trying to trick me now, they'd gone to some theatrical costume shop and gotten gray for their hair and padding for their bellies and rubber to create jowls, these very same people in my First Communion photo.

"You scared?" she said.

But I'd been lost in my thoughts and all I could give her was a dumb expression. "What?"

"Are you afraid?"

"Of what?"

"Look around."

"That's what I'm doing."

"In twenty years a lot of these people will be dead. Maybe even us."

"I know."

"It went so fast."

I was getting one of those seventh-grade erections, the kind you get but don't really want because it's embarrassing and you don't really know what to do with it. I was getting a seventh-grade erection there dancing in the darkness of our middle age.

"Why don't we go back to your apartment and go to bed?" she said. Her voice was curiously slowed. I wanted to attribute this to the incredible sexual sway I held over women but somehow I didn't think so.

I said, "You're drunk."

"No, I'm not. I only had two drinks tonight."

"Something pretty potent?"

"No, one of the pink ladies fixed me a Scotch and soda is all."

"Pink ladies?"

"Waitresses."

"Ah." And true enough, I had seen waitresses buzzing around. "They must have had some kind of incredible effect on you."

"Why?"

"You sound groggy."

"That's what's funny."

"What?"

"I sort of feel groggy, too."

"You want to sit down?"

"No, just hold me a little closer, will you?"

I sighed, pulled her closer. "Karen, I want you to tell me about the suitcase."

"Not now, all right?"

And she put her face into my shoulder and we danced as I once dreamed we would dance, eyes closed, even the tinny music melodic and romantic, and I felt her eminent sexual presence but also her odd vulnerability, and I held her for the girl she'd been and the woman she was, and I let my lips find her cheek and felt her finger tender on the back of my neck. And for a time, moving just like that in the Shamrock gym, in unison with all the people in our First Communion picture, I forgot all about Dr. Evans and how he'd been knocked out and forgot all about a curious figure in black on a black Honda motorcycle and all about a suitcase that nobody seemed to possess but that somebody seemed to want very, very badly.

I wasn't thinking of anything at all really, just floating on her perfume and the darkness and the music, and at first I was scarcely aware of how she began to slip from my arms to the floor.

"Karen?" I said. "Karen?"

People around us were looking and a few giggling, making the assumption she was drunk, but I didn't think so.

She was dead weight in my arms. And that was exactly what I thought: *dead weight.*

And then one of those quick bursts of panic, some sort of concussion, went off inside me and I heard myself shouting for lights up and for people to clear space and I knelt paramedic-style next to her feeling for pulse in neck and wrist, touching the tepid, sweaty skin of her body.

I found no pulse.

A priest and a fat man in a dinner jacket whom I

recognized as our class president came running up and said, "What's wrong here?"

"Ambulance," was all I could say, scarcely able to speak at all.

The overhead lights were on now and the magic was gone; you could see how old the floor was, and how beaten up the bleachers, and how cracked the tall windows. It was not the Stairway to the Stars of countless proms, after all. It was just a gym in a school more than half a century old and now in ill repair because the diocese saw no future in the Highlands. Nobody ever had.

She looked comic herself now, fake, the way the dancers had, fake gray tint in their hair, fake bellies, fake wrinkles and jowls and rheumy eyes, but what she was putting on was even more alarming because she was imitating death itself, like some phantom beauty from a Poe poem, but without the flutter of an eyelid or warm breath in her nostrils, not the faintest flicker in wrist or neck.

"Ambulance!" I shouted again, and this time I heard how ragged and desperate my voice had become and saw in the eyes of those encircling me a modicum of pity and a modicum of fear—both of her death and of the potential rage in my voice.

The priest, young as a rookie ballplayer, yet shorn of the grace that comes with age, knelt down beside me and said, "Maybe I'd best say some prayers with her." He didn't say "Last rites." He didn't need to. He produced a black rosary and began saying a "Hail Mary" and an "Our Father" and then a woman somewhere sobbed and for the first time I realized that the music had stopped, and that in the gym now there was just the rush and roar of time itself and nothing more, nothing more at all.

8 "You were the man dancing with her?"
"Yes."
"Can we talk a minute?"
"Sure."

Forty-five minutes had passed since the dance had ground to a nightmare halt, all motion seeming to be slowed down for a time, faces ripped open with tears and fear and the bafflement only death can inspire.

A white box of an ambulance sat with its doors open near the west entrance. The three people from the coroner's office had finished with her now, and two attendants in white, both with potbellies and hippie beards and eyes that had gazed on death perhaps too many times, had put her inside a black body bag, which was in turn put on a gurney that was now being loaded inside the well-lit confines.

Fanned around the ambulance were three hundred people from the dance. Many of the women had their husbands' coats draped over their shoulders. While the women were given to tears and occasional whispers, the men seemed doomed to an odd silence, gazing at the ambulance as if it explained some long-sought answer to a puzzle. There was a great deal of booze, punch from the bowl, Scotch in pint bottles, gin and vodka in flasks, beer in cans and big clear plastic cups. They'd been ready for a night when alcohol would set them free; now all alcohol could do was tranquilize them. Technically, there was a city ordinance against drinking out here, but none of the cops in the three white squad cars said anything. They just moved through the chill night, the stars clear and white in the dark blue sky, the scent of fir and pine and new grass contrasting with the smell of medicine and mortality coming from the ambulance.

"You're Dwyer, right?"

"Right."

"Used to be on the force?"

"Right."

"Thought so." He offered me a Camel filter. I shook my head. "I'm Bill Lynott, Benny McGuane's cousin."

"Oh. Right."

Benny McGuane was a sergeant in the Fourth Precinct and we'd been buddies back in our first years of directing traffic and chastising husbands who kept wanting to break the bones of their cowering little wives. In those days, that was all the law would let you do, chastise them. Maybe that's why Benny drank so much and maybe that's why he'd had such fragile success with AA, on and off the program every few months or so.

"How's he doing?" I said.

"Much better."

"Good."

"Think it's really going to work for him this time."

"He's a good man."

"He is that." He had some of his Camel filter, standing there next to me, his face like a psychedelic phantasm of the sixties, alternately red and blue in the whipping lights of emergency vehicles. He exhaled. "Shitty thing to happen at a reunion."

"Yes."

"You know her?"

"For a long time."

69

"You have any reason to think there was any foul play involved?"

"I don't think so."

He looked at me carefully. He had one those fleshy Irish faces you associate with monsignors whose secret passion is chocolate cake. "You don't sound sure."

There was the matter of the suitcase she'd wanted me to find. The matter of Dr. Glendon Evans being beaten up. The matter of her argument with Larry Price in the alley. The matter of somebody on a black Honda motorcycle following me around. "I guess I can't be sure."

"Any particular reason?"

"She was a woman who had a lot of friends and a lot of enemies."

"I just got a quick look at her. Damn good-looking woman."

"She was that, all right."

"You think I should call for a plainclothes unit?"

I thought about that one, too, and then I said, "I guess all we can do now is wait for the autopsy."

"That's twenty-four hours minimum."

"I know."

"If anything did happen here, aside from natural causes, I mean, that's a damn long wait. You familiar with poisoning victims?"

This kid was good. He must be taking all the night school courses available. That's one way you can divide cops these days. The men and women who put in their nighttime at the community colleges know a lot more than my generation of beat-pounders ever did.

"Somewhat."

"She look like she might have been poisoned?"

"No."

"You familiar with aneurysms?"

I shrugged. "Not really."

"Did she just slip into unconsciousness?"

"I guess. I'm not really sure. I mean, at first I thought she was just getting drunk."

"It might have been a stroke."

"Or a heart attack."

He sighed. "My old man always said not to count on anything and he was right." He snapped his fingers. "You can go just like that."

I was listening to him, sharing in his sense of how fragile our hold on living was, when out near the alley, next to a long silver Mercedes Benz sedan, I saw Larry Price grab a short, fleshy man and shake a fist at him. A tall, white-haired man with a Saint-Tropez tan and an arrogance that was probably radioactive stood nearby, watching. His name was Ted Forester. He was the man Glendon Evans had told me Karen was having an affair with. The man getting pushed around was a forlorn little guy named David Haskins. In high school the trio had been inseparable, though Haskins had always been little more than an adjunct, an early version of a gopher. Then, abruptly, Forester opened up the rear door of the Mercedes and Price pushed Haskins inside. A lot of people were watching all this, including Benny McGuane's cousin.

"What do you suppose that's all about?"

"I don't know," I said.

"Think I'll go find out."

By this time, Forester was in the car and behind the wheel. The headlights came on like eyes and the car surged forward. Bill Lynott put himself in front of the silver car, daring it to run him over.

He went over to the driver's side. I edged closer, so I could hear.

"What's the trouble here?"

"No trouble." Ted Forester was obviously not used to

answering the questions of some cop, of the uniformed variety yet.

"Why did you push that man into the car?"

"To be exact, Officer, *I* didn't push him into the car. My friend Larry Price pushed him into the car. And he did so because David Haskins, the man who is now snoring soundly in the back seat, got very drunk and obnoxious tonight. If, that is, it's any of your business."

"I'd like to see your license, please."

"What?"

Whatever powers the Supreme Court takes away from the police, a cop can always irritate you with his authority by asking to see your license.

"Your license, please."

"Why?"

"Because I have the legal authority to ask to see it and because I *am* asking to see it."

It was at this point that Ted Forester's eyes fell on mine and he frowned immediately. He glanced over at Larry Price, who nodded to him. I wondered if they were going to come after me in their big silver Mercedes. Then I wondered why they'd want to come after me in their big silver Mercedes.

Forester, tall, trim, handsome in the way of a bank president from central casting, took out a long slender wallet and opened it up like a diplomat presenting his credentials.

Billy Lynott, playing it out, took the wallet and shone his flash on the license and studied it as if he were going to be given a pop quiz on it.

Then he handed it back.

"All right, Mr. Forester," he said. "Just be sure to drive carefully."

Forester glowered at him and then at me again and then the Mercedes pulled out of the lot, Larry Price's eyes on me like lasers in the gloom.

"Asshole," Bill Lynott said when he came back to me. "He always was."

"Maybe I should have made him walk the line."

"He probably would have sued you."

"Yeah, he's the kind all right."

The ambulance attendants were closing the back doors and coming around to get in the cab.

For a moment I felt her in my arms again, the warmth of her flesh, the lovely smell of her hair, the unknowable mysteries of her gaze. I'd loved her and hated her and been afraid of her, but after it all, she'd still been the little girl I'd first met in kindergarten, shared a nap-time blanket with, watched grow into the beauty among the weeds and screams of the Highlands. Then I thought of the suitcase again. What was in it she'd wanted so badly? What was in it that somebody would beat up Glendon Evans for?

"Maybe you should get out of here," Billy Lynott said.

"Yeah. Maybe I should."

"I mean, if downtown wants to get a hold of you, they'll just give you a call."

"Right."

He put a hand on my shoulder. "I'll say 'hi' to Benny for you."

Suddenly, ridiculously, I wanted to see Benny again, have a beer or four with him, shoot some pool, speculate on women and the Cubs and why Democrats just always seemed better than Republicans. I didn't want to be nearing forty-five.

"Yeah," I said, "if downtown wants me, they can give me a call tomorrow."

I went and got in my Toyota and got out of there.

9 Donna wasn't there.

She has an apartment building you can get into only if someone inside buzzes you in.

I buzzed several times. Nothing.

I walked out to the parking lot and watched the moon and thought about Karen Lane, alternating between absolute certainty that what had happened to her had been coincidental—stroke, aneuryism, as Bill Lynott had suggested—and knowing with equal certainty that she'd somehow been murdered.

"Hello," said a couple walking past me from their car. They were both stockbrokers and both wore gray flannel suits, and both drove Datsun Zs and smoked Merits and belonged to health clubs and vacationed in Aspen and subscribed to the Book-of-the-Month Club. I knew all this because Donna had profiled them for *Ad World* as typical age-thirty-five consumers. The odd thing was, they even looked alike in a certain way, blond and blue-eyed, friendly in an almost ingenuous way. Their name was Burkett and I sort of liked them.

"Hello," I said. Then, "Say, would you let me into the building?"

"Sure," Todd Burkett said. "Is everything all right?"

"I think maybe Donna's just taking a shower or something. I was supposed to meet her here but there's no answer."

"Come on," Mary Anne Burkett said.

So we went up to one of the nine dark brick buildings piled against small mountains of pine and fine green grass that stretched along a river made silver by moonlight. As *Ad World* became more successful, Donna's apartments became fancier.

"We're having some stir-fry and white wine," Mary Anne said as we walked up the wide dramatic staircase leading to the second level. "Would you care to join us?"

"Then we're going to watch *Cape Fear* on the VHS. Have you ever seen it?"

"Yes," I said.

"Isn't Gregory Peck wonderful?" Mary Anne said.

Then I realized that no matter how much I liked them, there was some spiritual demarcation line that would always divide us. The picture belonged—cigars, boxer shorts, cheap straw fedora and all—to Robert Mitchum. Peck is in fact a cypher, little more than a symbol of all that is Right with Suburbia. Ethically, he's admirable as hell. Dramatically, he's as bland as an eighth-grade history teacher at a Fourth-of-July ceremony.

"No, thanks. But maybe some other time."

"Peck is really fantastic."

"Yeah, I know."

So they went to their woks and their Water Piks and their copy of *Cape Fear* and I went down to Donna's and knocked on the door.

I put my ear to the door the way private investigators who specialize in adultery always do. I heard all the sounds an apartment is supposed to make, the vague electronic buzz and crackle and hum that signify that all appliances are alive and doing well. But I heard nothing else.

Then down the hall I heard conversation and turned to see the Burketts talking to Candy James, a TV weather woman who lived in the apartment at the end of the hall. Candy was trying to get herself going in theater, too, and so we'd always just naturally gotten along. "Hi, Jack."

"Hi."

"I saw Donna leave a few hours ago. She said she was going over to your place."

But then she was supposed to come back here. "You didn't hear her come back?"

Candy, who is small and cute, with a curly cap of black hair and a smile that can melt metal, said, "No, I don't think so, anyway. You think something's wrong?"

"Probably not. I'm just kind of curious is all."

"Well, I've got a key. We swap keys in case we get locked out. You want it?"

"Great."

A minute later I had the key and went in and looked around and found nothing. As usual, the place was a tribute to work but not to tidiness, there being enough books and magazines stacked on the floors and on tables and on chairs to open a branch library. Unfortunately buried beneath all the *Ad World* research material were such gems as a drop-leaf harvest table with matching bird-cage Windsor chairs and a cast-iron mantel that she'd found in the city dump.

Her bed hadn't been made, there was yellow egg crust on the face of a green plate next to the microwave, the Crest tube in the bathroom looked as if it had been thrown into a trash compactor, then somehow lifted back out again (she has these killer moments of frugality).

Something was wrong. She is prompt, neurotically so, and if she said she'd meet me here, then she'd be here.

But she wasn't.

I went to the phone and stared out of the window at the silhouettes of the pines jagged against the night sky, their tips white in the moonlight. I let the phone ring at my place at least twenty times. Then I tried the offices of *Ad World* and got nothing and then I tried the number of her assistant, Jill, and got nothing there, either.

One thing about being paranoid is that you keep playing all these alternate scenarios out in your mind. The What-If game. I could reasonably assume she'd gone to my place. But that's all I could reasonably assume. Had she left there? If she hadn't, why wasn't she answering the phone? And that's when my paranoia kicked in and formed mental images of somebody on a black motorcycle, a Honda it was, and God alone knew what this person wanted. Or was capable of. I thought of Karen and how she had looked there at the last and then Karen's face became Donna's and something hard formed in the bottom of my stomach and I had one of those twitching spasms I used to get on the force just before I had to do something that scared me.

A rusted-out five-year-old Toyota is not necessarily built for speed, but I did a very slick job of setting a few Indy records on the way to my apartment.

10 You find my place in the inner part of the inner city, on a block where every house has stucco siding and a fair majority of the people you pass on the cracked sidewalks are probably armed. Donna, determined to make my efficiency apartment more "livable," had come over one day armed with draperies and slipcovers she'd bought at Sears, bright and nubby materials they'd been too, but after half an hour she'd dropped to the floor in a kind of semi-yoga position and said, "There just isn't any way to decorate around water stains on the wall, Dwyer. There just isn't."

The vestibule smelled of bleach, marijuana, beer, and Chinese food (there's a take-out place a block away).

I went up the stairs two at a time, now having worked myself into one of those states of stress the magazines always say give you at the least hemorrhoids and at the worst cancer, and then I pushed my key into the gold Yale dead bolt (the only thing in the house that's less than eighty years old). And then, groping for the wall switch, I stared deep into shadow.

"Come in and close the door, okay?"

The table lamp, the one with the beer-stained lamp shade, clicked on and there she sat.

Donna. Editor of *Ad World*. Sitting in the corner of a couch with a white bath towel pushed up against her head.

The towel was soaked with blood.

"God," I said. And for a moment that's all I could do. Just stand there and say over and over, "God." Half the time it was a prayer, the other half it was a curse.

"So you opened the door and then what?"

"So I opened the door and came in."

"And?"

"And nothing. I turned on the light and looked around and I thought, Boy, Dwyer's really got to get out of this place. I mean, I saw cockroaches again tonight. The size of Shetlands, Dwyer."

"Forget the cockroaches. What happened next?"

"I picked out a shirt and jacket and pair of pants from your closet."

"And then?"

"And then I went and used the biffy. Have you ever heard of Tidi Bowl, Dwyer?"

"Donna, are you going to tell me or what?"

"How I got hit on the head?"

"Right."

"Well."

"Why are you hesitating?"

"Because now that I think about it, I'm not sure I remember exactly." She touched a hand to the back of her head, the way Glendon Evans had earlier today. She wore a white blouse and gray tweed jacket and designer jeans. She has red hair and green eyes, one of which strays to a small degree, like Karen Black's (though I never mention Karen Black to her, Donna not thinking much of her acting), and she's one of those women who is very erotic in an almost offhanded way. (The only time she ever tried to be overtly sexy was when she got a baby-doll nightie, and I sort of spoiled it for her because her debut in the nightie coincided with Larry Holmes's title defense against Michael Spinks. She'd walked back and forth in front of the TV set about fifty times, so often I wondered if she wasn't doing some kind of aerobics, and finally she said, "Notice anything, Dwyer?" And all I'd said was, "Yeah, Larry looks old as shit." And then she'd walked out of the room and come back in and said, "Notice anything now, Dwyer?" She was completely naked.)

"You came out of the biffy," I said, leading her on like a prosecuting attorney.

"I came out of the biffy."

"And then he hit you."

She closed her eyes and thought a moment. "No."

"No?"

"No. I came out of the biffy and then . . ."

"And then?"

"Then I . . ." She thought a moment longer. "Then I leaned down to pick up your clothes where I'd rested them over the chair over there with just the one leg and then somehow she came up from behind me and hit."

"Wait a minute."

"What?"

"You said she."

"Yes."

"She?"

"Perfume. Very sweet perfume. So I assume it was a she."

"God."

"What?"

"A woman."

"Equal opportunity, Dwyer. No reason there can't be female thugs."

"All right. Anything else?"

"Just a weird sound."

"What kind of weird sound?"

"A kind of—creaking."

"Creaking? Like an old house?"

"No—creaking like . . ."

Then another paranoid image formed. "Creaking the way leather creaks?"

"Yes. Exactly. That's very good." She was getting excited.

The guy on the motorcycle with the black leather. It's a woman.

"Did she say anything?"

"No."

"God."

"What?"

"She wants the suitcase."

"What suitcase?"

"You hungry?"

"Was that an answer?"

"I just mean why don't we have a close look at your head and then if you seem to be all right, go have something to eat and then I'll tell you all about the suitcase."

"Dwyer."

"Yes."

"You haven't kissed me."

"I didn't want to hurt your head."

"You won't hurt my head. I mean I don't want a big lip lock or anything but just a nice discreet little kiss that says I care for you very much."

I took her hand. "How about if I tell you that I care for you very much and then I kiss you and kind of reinforce the message?"

"That would be nice."

So that's what I did. That's exactly what I did.

11 Most recording studios are designed to resemble expensive bomb shelters, tight as cocoons. Not only are the floors carpeted, so are most of the walls. Not only do the doors close tight, they are sealed along the edges. The baffling used to make the studios soundproof combines with somber indirect lighting to give the impression that even if Armageddon did come along, you'd never know about it inside here. You work in shadows, and the studio people seem to think this is just ducky, state of the art.

On the other side of a huge slab of glass, at a control panel the folks at "Star Trek" would envy, sat a very sleek guy with razor-cut hair and a mean black gaze and the kind of colorful, casual clothes that pass for southern Californian out here. He said, "Jack, I don't believe it. I mean, you're not coming across, you know?" He would take my six-second bit and mix it into the rest of the spot. Once he got me to read the way he wanted me to, anyway.

"Huh?"

"Look at the script, okay?"

I looked at the script.

"What does it say?"

"It says: 'If it wasn't for the home-equity loan I got at First National, I wouldn't have been able to send Timmy to college.'"

"Right."

"Well, you've got to sound grateful."

"Right. Sorry."

"You all right this morning?"

"Long night."

He grinned. "Chicks?"

"Nah."

"You know Betsy our receptionist?"

"Yeah."

"She thinks you're cute."

"Great."

"Really." He whispered over the intercom. "Take it from me, Jack. This chick knows things that'll make you blush. And take a gander at those gazongas. *Playboy* material or what?"

Steve, his name was, and at least the way he told it, he'd slept with no less than 50.7 percent of the women under age ninety-six in the city. But he had an annoying habit of never giving them any attributes but sexual ones. They were never smart or dumb or even pretty or ugly, they were always described only by the size of their breasts or various exotics tricks they seemed to know that nobody else had even heard of. (Over beers one night he'd mentioned a "Mexican sleeve job, you know, like in that 200 European Sexual Positions," and I had been left to ponder what that could mean—why Mexican? And what in hell could a "sleeve job" be?)

"You should try her," he said.

"Actually, I've got a friend."

"Oh, yeah. That ad chick. Man, nice-looking."

I guess I should have mentioned earlier that Steve is fifty-seven years old and a tribute to Grecian Formula. He works out not once, not twice, but three times a day, and confided to me once that he attributes his self-described "amazing virility" to massive doses of bee pollen ("I don't have to tell you about bees, do I, Jack?") He is also, for all his unctuous gonadic style, the best recording engineer and director outside of L.A. He takes advertising copy very, very seriously, knows how to make even the most unlikely lines play well, and the agencies are only too happy to send to his place, on a regular basis, big trucks loaded with green Yankee cash.

"You know how I see Jim—this guy you're playing?" he said.

"Uh-uh."

"Close your eyes. I'm going to paint you a picture."

"All right." I closed my eyes.

"He's forty-three years old. He lives in one of the suburbs. He's twenty pounds overweight, and no matter how hard he tries to diet, around eleven o'clock every night he sneaks down to the refrigerator where his wife has got this big sign that reads THINK BEFORE YOU EAT. Only he's so ravenous, he nearly rips the door off and then he just pigs out. Preferably on sweet stuff, but at this point he'll go for anything. He's disgusting to watch. You getting a picture?"

"I'm getting a picture."

"He goes to a Methodist church every Sunday but he nods off during the sermon. He wears Hush Puppies. During the sixties he got a college deferment so he didn't have to go to Nam but he didn't necessarily agree with all the people in the streets. But now this is the tricky part. He works for this corporation where their people are always getting fired. His boss is a real tyrant. Jim uses Valium and Maalox and Tums because inside he's a mess. He's losing his hair, and his erections aren't what they used to be, and even sending his only child to a state university is killing him financially. He's not shit, you seeing it?"

"I'm seeing it." And I was. "He eats because he's secretly depressed, right?" It was like acting class, fun, exhilarating, and only faintly embarrassing.

"Right."

"And maybe he and his wife don't really communicate much anymore, right?"

"Now you're flying, Jack."

"And he always feels that his back is to the wall, and that even the wall's going to cave in on him, right?"

"Exactly. And so, when First National gives him a home-equity loan, it's much more than just a loan—symbolically. Here's this fat guy in Hush Puppies who's this absolute piece of dust with his wife and with his boss—it's First National saying to this guy, Hey, we're your friend, pal. Other people may piss on you and spit on you and revile you with every dirty name imaginable—but not us, we're your *friend*, can you dig that—your friend? So what do we hear in his voice when he says, 'If it wasn't for that home-equity loan I got from First National, I wouldn't have been able to send Timmy to college'? What are we hearing, Jack?"

The bastard nearly had me in tears. "We're hearing gratitude because somebody finally gives a damn about this poor sad son of a bitch."

"That's exactly what we hear, Jack, and that's exactly what we want to hear from you. Gratitude. Because First National's your pal, your compadre, your best bud."

We got it in one take.

After the session, I went down the hall to the john and on the way I glanced out one of the few windows in the two-story facility to the parking lot where spring was struggling to paint everything green and crocus purple and crocus yellow and apple-blossom pink.

She was at the back of the lot, between a Pizza 2-U van and a large blue Buick. She just sat there and I wondered if she ever got hot inside those black leathers and that inscrutable black helmet, and then I wondered if she wore them for reasons of safety or because she liked the melodramatic edge they gave her.

But now it was time I found out not only who she was but what she wanted, so I went to the west end of the building and down the FIRE EXIT stairs and out the door. Being a cop got me in the habit of always carrying a ballpoint and a tablet that fit in the back pocket of my pants. I didn't need a gun right now. I needed the tablet.

The outdoor smelled of sunlight and diesel fuel and flowers. I wanted to be fishing. I worked my way along a line of cars in the lot until I came even with where she was, six cars over. There was an old woman apparently waiting for somebody in the doctor's office next door. She observed the way I sort of crouched down as

I moved. She frowned at me, not frightened in the least, but angry. She was probably going to turn me in.

I came up from behind the Pizza 2-U van and stood four feet from the motorcycle.

And then she turned, obviously sensing me somehow.

She'd had her engine running, so it was no trouble to do a fairly exotic wheelie and get out of there. The bike reared like a bronc, the long and curving lines of the woman in leathers as one with the metal itself, and then it came screeching and roaring down in contact with the pavement again and shot off in between a maze of parked cars.

There was no way I could catch her and I didn't intend to try.

But now I had her license number, and for now that was the only thing in the world I needed.

12 The Fourth Precinct was built back in the 1930s, when the then-Mayor had an architect for a son-in-law. A bad architect for a son-in-law. Which explains why Number Four looks like a cheesy papier-mâché set for a film set in mythical Baghdad. Built of concrete, it seems to be all minarets and spires and gargoyles, fanciful touches indeed for people named Mike O'Reilly and Milo Czmchek and Rufus Washington.

The interior of the Fourth resembles a big metro newspaper; desks butted up against each other, people running up and down the corridors between the desks, machines for coffee, sandwiches, pop, cigarettes, and newspapers lining the walls of the corridor leading to the rest rooms and the holding cells. Oh, yes, I should mention the para-bookmaking activities, too. At any given time, half the people in the Fourth, men and women alike, are laying down money on events of various descriptions, from the Cubs, Sox, Bears, to which local pols are finally going to get busted for (a) graft, (b) bestiality, or (c) general stupidity.

Somewhere in the welter of all this—the windows open wide to the spring and the cops daydreaming like fourth graders anxious to be outdoors—sat six-two Martin Edelman, my best friend and former partner. Today he was modeling one of his four Sears suits, the blue number, and one of the white shirts whose collar was blood-spattered from his shave this morning. (Even with a safety razor, he can commit atrocities Jack the Ripper could not have even conceived.) He has the sad blue eyes of a rabbi who has seen far too much of the world's nonsense and pettiness and cruelty, but then there is his smile, which is curiously innocent and open, if only occasionally on view. His brown toupee was on slightly crooked, but I saw no point in telling him. It is always on crooked.

A cop named Manning leaned in just as I started to put my hand on Edelman's shoulder. "You in for the Cubs?"

"How much?" Edelman said.

"Ten."

"Jeeze."

"Ten, Edelman. You won twenty last week. Maybe you'll win forty this week."

Edelman, taking out his wallet, said, "The way you hustle people, Manning, you should be an insurance salesman."

Manning said, "You forget, Martin. I *was* an insurance salesman."

"Oh, yeah."

"You got the Cubbies and two points," Manning said, and vanished.

Edelman started to go back to his typewriter—he does very well with two fingers, very well—when I said, "Someday one of the TV stations is going to do a story on all the betting cops do."

He turned around and showed me his smile. He always manages to make me feel as if seeing me is the most special thing that's happened to him in a week. And I always hope it is.

"Dwyer, hey."

"Hey, Martin."

We shook hands and I just looked at him. In some odd way he's my brother, and I knew this the day we first met years ago back at the Academy when neither of us could shinny up a rope worth a damn. These days, we even share the same problems—we both need to do exactly the same things: lose ten to fifteen pounds, use a few more quarts of Visine a week, and try to convince ourselves that the sky is not going to fall in within the next twenty minutes.

"You hear Manning? I won forty last week." He sounded young saying it and it made me feel good.

"So what did you do with it?"

"You really want to know?"

"Yeah."

"Bought Parkhurst from Number Three a lunch I've owed him for a while, got some new Odor Eaters, bought a new band for my Timex, and then gave the rest of it to my son for a ball glove."

"Nothing's changed."

"Huh?"

"All the excitement."

He laughed. "Asshole." Then he picked up a pink phone slip and said, "I got a note this morning that you were going to be calling me about an autopsy."

"Right."

"Well, I've got some preliminary results." His fingers searched through several layers of paper and then he came up with it. "This is just what I took over the phone. You read my writing okay?"

"I'll try." Edleman's handwriting is a form of communication that would stump even the people who translate cuneiform.

So I looked at it and said, "Natural causes?"

"Yeah. You think it was going to be something else."

"I had some suspicions along those lines."

"Sorry."

"Librium and alcohol."

"Kills a lot of people."

"They going to rule it a suicide?"

He shrugged. "You know how it goes. Most of the time they try to spare the families and just say 'natural causes.' From what I gather, there was no note and the officer's report said you didn't find her particularly upset or depressed."

"I guess not."

"Sorry."

"Yeah."

"You don't believe it?"

"I'm not sure yet." Then I remembered the tablet in my back pocket. "How about running a number for me?"

"This got anything to do with Karen Lane?"

"Probably."

"Probably." He smiled. "Probably." He held out his hand and tore off the sheet of paper with the number on it and then turned around and picked up the phone.

While we were waiting, he said, "I assume if there's anything of interest in this for the police, you'll let us know right away."

"Of course."

"Why don't I believe you?" he said and started doodling on a lined pad. The phone still cupped to his ear, he said, "You and Donna set a date yet?"

"Not yet."

"I read this article on stress the other day. In the paper."

"I read it, too." Edelman wants me to get married.

"Married people have less stress," he said. And then into the phone, "Okay, ready."

He wrote it down, name and address, and then hung up and handed me the paper. "So how about it?"

"How about what?"

"She's a wonderful woman and I can tell just by looking at her that she wants to get married."

I straightened his toupee for him and said, "We'll call you the minute we decide, Edelman. The minute."

I turned to leave and he said, "That license number I ran through for you. You into anything I should know about?"

"Not yet, Martin. Not yet."

Then I left the station and went to look up a Mrs. Patti Slater.

13 You might mistake the Windmere Home for one of those piss-elegant motels all gussied up to resemble a seventeenth-century manor house. It isn't, of course, it's an old folks' home, or whatever it is we're calling people over seventy these days. The grounds revealed a great deal of brick and concrete and very little foliage or trees or grass. The east windows looked out on a parking lot and the west on the brick face of a natural-wood doctor's complex and the north windows on a vacant lot with a big FOR SALE sign. Grim, when you considered that many of the people herein had come here to die. Probably even daytime television was preferable to staring out a window that only revealed either other buildings or dinosaur-like semis chugging up the broad avenue outside.

The reception area continued the motel motif, a long waist-high counter running across most of a big, carpeted room that contained enough fake wood furniture and Starving Artist paintings to send the owners of Holiday Inn into sinful ecstasy.

Seated in one of the chairs was a palsied old lady whose twisted hands rested on a black cane and whose aged eyes stared mournfully at the death the chipper people who'd brought her here were trying cheerfully to deny to her. She wore a prim dark suit with a large brooch at the throat of her prim white blouse.

"She'll love it here," said a plump woman with hair tinted a color God had never invented. She wore a white nurse's uniform and smiled with formidable dentures.

"Did you hear that, Mother?" shouted a thin man with rimless glasses and a bald head. He wore a blue jogging suit and white Reeboks. The woman with him, presumably his wife, was dressed similarly. Were they going to head right for the track, as soon as they'd dumped the old lady off?

"We believe in keeping people active, that's one thing that makes Windmere so special," said the nurse, sounding like a living brochure. "We have a Jacuzzi and we play bingo four nights a week, and the community theater sends singers over several afternoons a month."

But the old lady wasn't going to be kidded. She clung to her cane as if it were life itself and stared down the hole they were about to push her in. I wanted to go over and sit next to her and put my arm around her and say something comforting, but what would I say when it came right down to it? That I was sorry she was pushing off, that I didn't want her to push off, that I hoped her son and daughter-in-law tripped all over their Reeboks?

"I'll get Ken," the nurse said.

Ken proved to look like a member of the Chicago Bears blitz circa mid-sixties. He wore a white T-shirt and white ducks and white socks and white canvas shoes and his gray hair was burr-cut and he'd shaved his fleshy face so smoothly it was as pink as a baby's. He had eyes like lasers and biceps you could rest refrigerators on. He also surprised the hell out of me by making the old lady not only look up for the first time but actually smile. He extended his arm and said, "Is this my date for the evening?"

"Don't I wish," the old lady said, and her voice cracked in real laughter.

So Ken led her off. Son and daughter-in-law signed some papers and started to leave and then the daughter-in-law turned back once to the hall where the old lady had disappeared on Ken's arm and then looked around and said, "You really think this is the right thing, David?"

"Honey, we have to be realistic."

Then she nodded and glanced down at her Reeboks and then they were gone, leaving his mother to the dubious balm of amateur entertainers and bingo.

I went over to the nurse. "I'd like to see Mrs. Slater, please."

She was now behind the counter and doing some very deft things with a computer keyboard.

She looked at me. "It's Wednesday."

"Yes, isn't it?"

"Visiting afternoons are Monday, and Friday."

So I went into one of my routines. I put out my hand and she didn't really have any choice but to take it and I said, "I'm Frank Evans and I'm her nephew from Omaha. I sell plumbing supplies and I was just driving through the city, so I thought I'd stop and say hi to her."

Not that I understood any of this, of course, why a black Honda motorcycle that could do maybe 150 miles per hour flat-out would be registered to a woman in a nursing home.

"Gosh," the woman said.

"What?"

"It'd really be a hassle."

"Really?"

"Yes. I mean, well, people aren't always ready to be shown at the drop of a hat."

"Shown" being the operative word here. I had the impression that they lined them up in their wheelchairs and hosed them off to get rid of the stench, then brought in an industrial waxer to shine pallor and wheelchair alike. Then they shot them up with enough Thorazine to make Charles Manson mellow for the rest of his life. And then they brought in the guests and moved them along quickly, the way you got moved along quickly in an art gallery where an especially popular artist was being shown, and the visitors got to see how clean and shiny and docile their parents looked and so the most wonderful thing of all happened.

They could jump back in their Volvos, throw in some Barry Manilow tapes, and drive back to suburbia without feeling even 1.4 percent guilty.

"Gosh," she said. "I'm afraid it's impossible. You know, we really do try to be accommodating here at Windmere, but—" She was too plump and wore too much makeup, but still you could see the erotic twenty-year-old she'd probably been, the full lips especially knowing. But she ruined any real human heat with the living brochure monotone of her voice. She shrugged and her breasts raised slightly against the fabric of her bra and the bra in turn against the fabric of her white uniform and it was one of those odd moments—sunlight on linoleum, the smell of floor wax, a robin on a window ledge—when the thought of sex should not have occurred at all but it did. Oh yes, it did. But her green eyes held no promise, and so my erection slunk away.

"Has my cousin been here?"

"Cousin?" she said.

I smiled my glad-hander smile. "I imagine you'd know my cousin. Rides a motorcycle."

Now she smiled, too. "Oh, Evelyn Dain."

"That's right. Evelyn Dain."

"No, she comes Mondays and Fridays." The green eyes were haughty a moment. "The hours everyone else does."

"I should talk to her, I guess. About Patti. See how things are going." Here I had to be careful. Careful and casual. "You wouldn't know where she works, would you? I seem to recall she changed jobs a while back."

The phone rang, helping me. If the nurse had any doubts about me, about who I might really be and what I might really be doing there, they were forgotten in the rush of answering the phone. "Damiano's Aerobics over on Third Avenue."

"Thanks," I said. "And say hi to Patti for me."

She smiled with those wonderful erotic lips—you imagined them the kind of lips sixteenth-century kings demanded in their whores—and then waved me off to take her phone call. After answering, she said, "I'll be glad to tell you about Windmere." She was back to being a brochure.

14 "How's your head?" I asked Donna.

"Pretty good. As long as I don't move too fast. She really hit me. Where're you?"

"Phone booth across the street from an aerobics place out on Third Avenue."

"You're joining an aerobics class?"

"No, the woman who hit you. It's where she works."

"God," she said. "That's neat."

"What's that?"

"That you've found her already. I mean, you really are a good detective."

"All I did was run down a couple of things."

"But that's what's so neat, Dwyer. You run down a couple of things and bingo, you've got it."

"That's just the problem."

"What?"

"I don't know what I've got."

"How come?"

"Well, the motorcycle is registered to a Mrs. Slater who resides at the Windmere nursing home. I don't know what relation she has to this Evelyn Dain or why Evelyn Dain is following me or what any of this has to do with the suitcase that Karen Lane hired me to find."

"Yeah, God, it really is confusing, isn't it?"

"Yeah."

"So why're you doing it? I mean, why not just tell Edelman?"

"Because right now the police are saying that Karen Lane's death was an accident resulting from mixing alcohol and barbiturates. Which means they won't be pursuing things. Which means it's left to me, I guess."

"I wouldn't mind if you, you know, sort of paid her back for me."

"Who?"

"Evelyn Dain."

"Paid her back?"

"You know."

"You mean hit her?"

"Not hit her, exactly."

"What's 'exactly' mean?"

"You know, sort of trip her or something."

"Trip her?"

"That wouldn't be so bad. She wouldn't get hurt but she'd get the point."

I laughed. "It would be a lot easier if you'd just look her up and hit her yourself."

Now she laughed. "Be serious. I've never hit anybody before, Dwyer, except my older sister Ellen, and the one time I did it my mother grounded me for the weekend and I had to miss the Herman's Hermits concert."

"You liked Herman's Hermits?"

"I admit he couldn't sing but he was cute."

"If I get half a chance, I'll trip her."

"But not hard, all right? Just kind of a, uh, regular trip, you know?"

"Right. One regular trip coming up."

"I miss you."

"I miss you, too."

So then I went into the Hardees across the street from the small concrete building with the three store-front windows, one of which belonged to a Penny Saver shopper, one to an appliance store, and the third to the aerobics place. Inside that window you could see maybe twenty women doing exercises as grueling as anything I'd ever done at the Academy.

Knowing what was ahead of me—a stakeout and a long one—I self-pitied myself into justifying a double-decker hamburger, fries, and a vanilla shake. Stakeouts demand a lot of energy.

Loaded down with a white bag smudgy with grease, I went back to my Toyota, turned on the FM to a call-in show where people were arguing about whether condom advertising should be permitted on the air (AIDS was rearranging the American way of life), and proceeded to sit there for the next four and a half hours, watching both the storefront and the gleaming black Honda motorcycle in the adjacent parking lot.

This was a neighborhood in transition. In my boyhood days this had been the best section of town you could live in if your parents were working class, Irish, Italian, and Czech mostly, and every day on the sunny walks proud men in dungarees strolled to work, black lunch pails smelling of bologna sandwiches dangling from one hand, and a local newspaper they loved to curse in the other. You dreamed Plymouth dreams in those days (it had been one of my old man's fondest fantasies to pull up in front of the family house in a new 1955 baby blue Plymouth) as you moved away from the Highlands down here and as you gradually began to realize that, thanks to government loans and your parents' frugality, you were going to be the first generation that got to go to college.

But I didn't know what kind of dreams they dreamed here now. Sixteen-year-old girls pushed strollers past my car now, and your first impression was that they were the infants' sisters but in fact they were the infants' mothers. Scruffy boys in black leather jackets with tattoos on their knuckles and a cigarette hack bothering their throats already came by, too, and old men who gave the air of just wandering. Old women clutching small bags of groceries hurried on looking scared. And bored cops, tired of all the bullshit—and, man, you just don't know how much bullshit beat-cops get laid on them day in, day out—watched it all, just wanting to get back to their tract homes and watch the Cubbies or watch their kids or watch their wives or watch any goddamn thing except this neighborhood get even meaner.

Dusk came and I had to take the risk of running into the Hardees can and emptying my bladder and running back out. I had a splotch on my crotch where, in my haste putting it back in, I'd dribbled. But the motorcycle was still there. The lurid neons at the Triple-X Theater down the street came on and then all the taverns lit up and this big annoying mechanical bear on top of a car wash started waving like King Kong to passing motorists. Several of them had the good sense to flip him the finger.

I watched the ladies and tried to figure out if the somewhat angular blonde leading the class was the woman I wanted. Possibly. But just as possibly she could be the manager, out of sight in some back office. My car stank of fried food. I wanted, in order, to talk to my seventeen-year-old son (who had started missing school lately, going through some kind of teenage funk), Donna, Glendon Evans (to question him more carefully about some of the things Karen Lane had said to him during their time of cohabitation), and Thomas Merton, the Trappist monk-poet whose books I'd been reading lately, to find out just how he'd managed to deal with all the craziness.

Then, around eight o'clock, my bottom very tired, my eyelids getting heavy, the women started filing out of the aerobics center. Their chatter was like bright birds on the soft night air and I liked listening to it. It was happy and human and hopeful, proud as they were of their workout and the good way they felt about themselves at this moment.

Then the lights inside the aerobic center went out.

I sat up straight and turned on my engine.

Then I sat there for twenty minutes, wasting a couple dollars' worth of gas.

Being a paranoid, I began to wonder if she had seen my car and simply gone out the back door, leaving her bike so I'd sit here all night like a very stupid rent-a-cop watching it.

Around eight thirty-five, she came out.

I still couldn't get a good look at her because she was back in her leathers again. She even had the helmet on. She looked like a superheroine in a comic book.

Without looking around, without hesitating, she went over to the parking lot, mounted the bike with a physical economy that spoke of the condition she was in, and then, moments later, took off.

I took off after her, having no idea whatsoever where she was going.

15 The old money built their homes east, on hills that formed a ragged timberline back when the only certain means of transportation other than walking had been the Conestoga wagon. They built east and they built big and they built conservative, brick and stone and wood, hammered and chiseled and curved to imitate the Victorian style. It was through this section of hills she led me, dips steep as roller coasters, peaks from which you could see the electric sprawl of the city beneath. Occasionally a timid deer came to the edge of the road, then disappeared, frightened, back into the pine and hardwood acres posted NO HUNTING. There were gates in the gloom, big iron gates, usually painted black, beyond which lay curving asphalt roads and then the houses themselves. Forty-five minutes had gone by. The temperature had dropped ten degrees, from early spring to late winter. The one thing the Toyota did well, besides rusting, I mean, was kick out heat. I was snug as a baby in the womb. I just didn't know where the hell she was taking me. Two thoughts kept crisscrossing: Was she aware of me and simply driving me around and around or did she just like to go for rides after work, the way I sometimes did?

Then she veered southeast, and we came into the section new money had built, lying below us in grassy foothills. From up here you could see down into their backyards with their inevitable swimming pools and inevitable tennis courts and inevitable sprawling flag-stone patios. The style of the houses changed from Victorian to everything from French Provincial to Colonial to Mediterranean. In the night now they seemed to glow with prosperity, gods perched above the moaning masses below. You could hear dogs bark in the darkness and you knew they would not be pretty collies or cute Scotties. They'd be Dobermans or maybe even (this was the fashion this season) pit bulls. These days, with people standing in cheese lines two blocks down from where factories stood unused, these days the gods had damned well better get themselves some protection.

I kept a city block behind her, but even so she pulled off the road so abruptly, I nearly had to put the car into the ditch. I cut the lights. Waited.

She'd cut her own lights. For a time I couldn't pick her out in the starry blackness.

I felt awkward, foolish, trapped. Apparently she'd been on to me all along and was now waiting for me to make my own move. Turn around and go back the other way? Stroll up to her and ask her just who the hell she was and why she'd knocked out my girlfriend and most likely a shrink named Evans?

At first I couldn't tell if my eyes were only playing tricks or if she had actually just done what she'd seemed to.

Left her black Honda and started walking down the road.

I reached up and popped the lid off the dome light and then thumbed out the bulb. I didn't want my car to light up when I eased out of it.

I put one foot down on the road and smelled the chill piny night and then put a second foot down and watched the way rolling cumulus clouds covered the quarter moon. She was ahead of me somewhere, walking. But where? And why?

I went after her, keeping to the side of the road, where even the gods had to put up with empty beer cans and Hershey wrappers and Merit packages soggy with dew.

On my right the pines were solid, broken only occasionally by small clearings of grass, still dead and brown. The left held two homes set very far back, little more than lights glimpsed through the hardwoods. Hearing a car behind me, I turned my head to the left so the driver couldn't see my face. He turned into the opposite drive, a chunky silhouette in a red BMW.

Then I saw her.

She was crawling up the face of two steep iron gates with the acumen of a monkey showing off for Sunday-afternoon visitors. She was so good at it, I just stood and watched her, forgetting for a moment why I was here in the first place. In her black leathers, she was hard to see. Then she dropped down on the other side of the gate, her body making a small sound as it touched the asphalt, and then she vanished.

I walked the rest of the way over to the iron gates. The estate was surrounded by a large stone wall. Schlepping up the gates was probably easier than going over the stone wall.

Just behind me was a country-style mailbox. I went over and hauled out my flash and looked to see the name.

I stood there a moment and contemplated what the hell it could mean. Things had come abruptly together here. Yet, at the same time, nothing had come together at all.

The name on the mail box was LARRY PRICE, the same Larry Price who had been my high school classmate, the same Larry Price I'd gotten into a fight with during senior year, and the same Larry Price who had mysteriously been arguing with Karen Lane out in the alley the night she'd died.

Why would the woman in black leathers be coming to see Larry Price?

Another car swept past. I jumped into brush on the side of the intricately patterned iron gates. It hurtled on into the gloom.

I put my hand to the rough surface of stone. In movies, guys are always vaulting over walls like this one—it couldn't have been much higher than seven feet—or shinnying up them with rope ladders. But unfortunately, I had never been able to list vaulting or shinnying among my useful skills.

Hoping for blind luck, I went over to the gate and put my fingers through the bars and tried to see if they might not magically come apart and let me just sort of amble right on in. But there would be no ambling.

There would be only vaulting or shinnying.

So I put my right foot in the gate and proceeded to climb. I just hoped nobody was watching, especially the woman in black leathers. I had this image of her sitting somewhere in the bushes inside the estate laughing her shapely ass off.

It couldn't have taken longer than two or three hours to get over the gate and land—as in crash-landing—on the other side. All the way, between sweating, groaning, and cursing, I kept promising to enroll myself in some sort of mercenary school and learn how to do stuff like this. As a cop, the most strenuous thing I'd ever had to do was chase a a car thief two blocks. He had done me the favor of being at least fifty pounds overweight.

I stood on the other side breathless and soaked, panting and cursing still. And then I looked around at the estate fanning out before me. The asphalt road wound up past steep copses of pines and then wound back again to grounds that displayed a gazebo almost luminescent in the moonlight and a tennis court canvas-covered for the cold months and a small hothouse appearing almost secretive, tucked as it was into a stand of hardwoods.

The house, not as big as you might expect, was a garrison-style Colonial, two-stories, an off-yellow. To the west was a three-stall garage. All the doors were open. There were no cars. I glanced back at the house. Darkness. Stillness. Nobody home.

But she was in there somewhere. My motorcycle rider.

Taking a deep breath, hefting my flashlight as a weapon the way cops do, I started toward the house. If she'd found a way in, I'd find a way in. And then I'd confront her and find out all the things I needed to know, and maybe then I'd stumble onto the suitcase Karen Lane had hired me to find.

I was halfway to the house when she hit me. She got me from behind and she got me clean and I don't think I even had time for one good obscenity before the back of my head seemed to crack open and before I automatically put my hands out to soften my collision with the ground.

16 The back of my head hurt and the front of my head hurt and the side of my head hurt. There was a terrible taste in my throat and I needed to pee. Badly. The way you do when you wake at 2 A.M. from a night's drinking. I lay in a cluster of dead leaves over which a sheen of frost sparkled silver in the moonlight. My hand, for no reason I could understand, clutched a brittle brown pine cone.

I began the careful process of getting up, trying to gauge if I'd been hit hard enough to suffer a concussion, and wondering vaguely where the closest emergency hospital was.

The first thing I did was take care of my bladder. I leaned my left hand against a hardwood for support and then let go, the yellow stream raising steam and making a hard constant noise on the last of autumn's leaves. Then I took out my handkerchief and began daubing it against the back of my head. There was only a small smudge of blood on the white fabric when I held it out for appraisal. Despite a headache, I did not seem to be hurt badly. My watch said nine-fifteen. I'd been out less than fifteen minutes.

In the west wing of the house, on the second floor, I saw the arc of a flashlight splash across a pinkish wall, and then go dark. She was inside now. Busy. I wasn't going to let her get off easily. Not at all. I thought of Donna's joke—couldn't I trip the lady in leather just a little bit? I was going to trip her a whole lot.

I moved awkwardly at first, staggering a bit like a stereotypical drunk, but gradually I got used to the headache and moved with a little less trouble. When I reached the front yard, which was defined by severe flattop hedges on both east and west ends, I went up to the oak front door and tried the knob.

Locked.

I put my ear to the door. Faintly I heard the hum and thrum of a house at rest but nothing else.

I went around to the rear, to the area between the garage and back door. It was cold and my head still hurt, but I was angry with her now and I was damn well going to get to express my anger.

I tried the knob on the back door. It turned easily. I went inside, up three steps covered with a rubber runner, and into one of those open kitchens with a huge butcher-block table like a sacrificial altar in the center, and pots and pans hanging from a suspension above. They gleamed in the moonlight falling golden through the mullioned windows. I smelled paprika and cocoa and coffee. I smelled thyme and mustard seed and basil. They were feminine smells and pleasant and I wanted to stand there for hours and float on them the way I used to float on marijuana. Contact high is the term I wanted, I think.

Upstairs she bumped a piece of furniture and it was loud as a truck overturning. She was searching for something, apparently, and apparently searching desperately.

I wrapped my hand around my flashlight and proceeded through a house with accents of bricks and brass, with beams over the living room, and crown moldings everywhere. The furnishings ran to Early American but I don't mean the stuff you see in suburban furniture stores. I'm talking, among others things, two items of special note: fan-back Windsor chairs and a Chippendale mahogany slant-top desk, items antique hunter Donna would get goofy about. I'd always known that Larry Price had come from a wealthy family; I just hadn't known how wealthy.

A sweeping staircase curved up into the darkness at the top of which two long narrow windows let in light.

I moved as quietly as I could up the stairs. At the top I smelled perfume from the master bedroom that lay thirty feet away. An eighteenth-century walnut longcase clock tocked the time. I looked down the hall.

Light from her flash shone in a room at the end of the hall, between door and jamb.

The clock covered any noise my tiptoe steps might have made. I was going to go in fast and make no concessions just because she was female. I was going to trip the hell out of her.

The door was open maybe three inches. I raised my foot to kick it in.

But I didn't have to. She yanked it open for me.

And then stood there with a very fancy silver-plated .45 in her hand and said, "You bastard. I should kill you right here."

17 Five minutes later, me sitting on a couch in a den filled with the sort of leather-bound classics nobody ever actually read and enough leather furniture to please the richest lawyer in the land, she threw my wallet back at me.

"Who the hell are you?" I said.

She just shook her head and went over and sat very efficiently on a broad leather ottoman. Her bottle-blond hair was almost white against the black leather of her riding suit. For the first time, her helmet gone, I could see her face, the broad, lopsided mouth, the earnest blue eyes, the freckles that somehow made her seem younger than the lines around her mouth and eyes indicated she was.

She put her head down, like an athlete who has just

finished a long run, but the one time I squirmed to lift weight off one buttock and put it on the other, her head snapped up and she pointed the .45 in the approximate vicinity of my forehead.

Then she put her head back down again and it was then I sensed it, that certain but special air the insane exude. I'd experienced it once while visiting a cop friend on a psych ward, felt it in the vivid stares that followed me with both fear and ferocity, in the curious inexplicable smiles some odd gesture would suddenly evoke. You feel sorry for them but they scare you, too—like a sick dog you come upon, wanting to help him, but fearful he might be rabid.

She raised her head and said, "He killed Sonny. He was one of them, anyway."

"What?"

She spoke with the kind of fragile gentleness you associate with poor but honorable spinsters. "Isn't my English clear, Mr. Dwyer?"

"What I guess you said is, 'He killed Sonny.'"

"That is in fact what I said, Mr. Dwyer."

"Well, I've got a couple of questions about that."

"Which are?"

"First of all, who is the 'he' you're referring to, and second, who is Sonny?"

The blue eyes grew grave. She sat there looking old suddenly, and tender too, and something like a chill worked down my back, and I felt afraid of her. It wasn't the gun, it was her simple flat connection to some truth I did not understand, the ageless mad truth of the fanatic.

"You know who 'he' is, Mr. Dwyer, and you certainly know who Sonny is. That's why you want the suitcase. So you can sell it to the men who killed him."

Then she very carefully got up and, even sensing

what she was going to do, all I could do was sit and watch, fascinated as much as frightened.

She got me just once, but it was a good clean hit with the butt of the .45 right on the edge of my jaw. The headache, which had waned, came back instantly. It was now joined by something very much like a toothache.

I started to move, my male arrogance instinctively believing that I could simply grab her fragile wrist and throw her to the floor, but she had other ideas.

She put the cold, oil-smelling weapon right to my temple and said, "I'm going to make you a deal, Mr. Dwyer."

"What deal?" I wanted to sound hard, even harsh, giving her the impression that even though I had a mouth full of blood and the world's biggest ice-cream headache, I was still in charge here. I was a man, and dammit, men were always in charge of women, right? Even women with guns. Right?

"I won't kill your girlfriend if you get the suitcase and bring it to me at ten o'clock tomorrow night. I'll phone you where I want you to bring it. Do you understand me?"

I started to snarl something about what I'd do if she so much as looked at Donna again, but for the second time that night, the tall, slender woman in the black motorcycle leathers caught me fast and cracking sharp across the back of the head.

This time I fell into the darkness with something like relief. My head was starting to ache intolerably and I was tired and confused and at least a little bit afraid of what I saw in her blue eyes, the same thing I'd seen one night ten years earlier when a young mother had put an ice pick through the eyes of her infant and then waited patiently for the policeman she'd summoned. I had been that policeman.

18 Next morning I woke up with Donna sitting on the edge of my bed in a royal blue belted robe and her beautiful wild red hair fresh from the shower. I was in her bed in her apartment, where I'd come in a stupor not unlike drunkenness after leaving Larry Price's house, where the woman in black had knocked me out not once but twice.

"How're you feeling?"

"Better than I should, probably," I said.

"This should help."

I sat up in bed like an invalid and she set the tray across my lap. There were two lovely eggs over easy on a pink plate. And two lovely pieces of delicately buttered toast. And three lovely orange slices. And a lovely steaming cup of coffee. And two round little white tablets that unfortunately were not half as lovely as the other things on the plate.

"Aspirin," she said. "I figured you'd need them." She bent over and gave me a soft kiss and I just held her there momentarily, knowing her for the prize she was.

"Thanks," I said.

Her bedroom was a woman's room, with yellow walls and canopied bed, and outsize stuffed animals, one I like especially, a plump bear with oddly forlorn eyes and a little red cap. He sat in the corner, his arms forever spread in greeting, watching me eat, which I did with boot-camp hunger.

"Man," I said.

"Taste good?"

"Tastes great."

"Boy, I love to watch you eat."

"I thought you said I needed to lose ten pounds."

"You do. But I still love to watch you eat. It just makes me feel—secure somehow."

She leaned over and gave me a kiss again and then she said, "May I tell you something?"

"Sure," I said, wiping up egg yolk with the last piece of toast. I let my gaze lie on the windows, blue with cloudless spring sky. A jay flitted past the window and perched on a branch just blooming. The window was partly opened. I thought of how fresh laundry smelled in the breeze.

"That woman's threats last night?"

"Yes."

"I'm scared, Dwyer."

I put my hand out and brought her over to me. She sat on the edge of the bed. She smelled of perfume, bath soap, and clean skin. She smelled wonderful.

"I want you to go to Joanna's for a few days," I said.

"What?"

"Please."

"Joanna? You think I could handle it for a few days? All those heartbreak stories?"

Joanna was a newswriter at a TV station, a woman gifted not only with talent but great looks that did not seem to do her much good with men. She was perpetually heartbroken.

"I really wish you'd call her," I said.

"What about you?"

"I'll stay at my place. I'll be all right."

She touched my head. "Dwyer, she's mean. So far she's knocked out three people, and from what you say, she's not hinged quite right."

"I know." Then I smiled. "All the more reason for you to stay at Joanna's. You've got the magazine done for the month. You can just sort of hole up. What I'd like you to do is pack a bag now and leave. And watch your rearview very carefully."

"Make sure nobody is following?"

"Right."

"God, people really do do that, don't they? I mean, it's not just in detective movies, is it?"

"No, it isn't."

"What're you going to do?"

"Check the calls on my answering service. Then I'm not sure."

She picked up the tray. "Did you really like it?" She's very insecure about her cooking, probably because her former husband Chad was always criticizing her for her lack of culinary imagination and, by implication, her lack of culinary skills.

"Honey, it was great, and it was sweet. It was very sweet."

"Thanks for saying that."

"It's the truth."

Water ran in the kitchen sink; then the bathroom door closed; then the hair drier erupted. I phoned my service. This was my day off at American Security, so my first dread was that there'd be a message saying somebody hadn't shown up so would I please come in. Fortunately, no. The only message came from a Dr. Allan Cummings. I wrote his number down and thanked the woman picking up the calls this morning. Just before we hung up, she said, "I saw one of your commercials on the tube last night. You did a good job."

"Thanks."

"Oh, that doctor who called?"

"Yes."

"He sounded real—uptight or something."

"Thanks."

"Sure."

We hung up. I dialed Dr. Cummings' number. These days, getting through directly to a doctor is nearly as unlikely as winning a lottery. So I was surprised when a baritone male voice said, "Dr. Cummings here." He must have given me a direct number.

"Doctor, my name is Jack Dwyer."

"Oh yes, Mr. Dwyer, thanks for returning my call." He sounded nervous.

Then he stopped talking. I sensed hesitation.

"What can I do for you, Doctor?"

"Well, I was wondering if we might talk a few minutes."

"Of course."

"What I have reference to, Mr. Dwyer, is the story in the newspaper this morning."

"I see."

"The one about Karen Lane dying of an accidental overdose of Librium and alcohol."

"Yes."

"Well, the story said that you were with her at the time of her death and that you were a former policeman, so I thought I would tell you something that might be pertinent."

"What's that, Doctor?"

"Karen Lane was my patient for several years. I'm a medical doctor, not a psychiatrist, but for some of my patients who tend to get depressed or overanxious, I prescribe various kinds of tranquilizers or antidepressants."

"I see."

"The point I'm trying to make here, Mr. Dwyer, is that I once prescribed Librium for her."

"And?"

"And she had an allergic reaction to it. Welts appeared on her tongue and her throat got very red and sore."

I threw my feet over the side of the bed. It was one of the moments I wanted a cigarette. "So what are you saying?"

"I'm not sure what I'm saying, Mr. Dwyer. I wish I could say absolutely that Karen Lane would never take Librium, but sometimes, as we get older, our allergies change. We begin to tolerate things we once couldn't tolerate—and vice versa."

"When was the last time you saw her, Doctor?"

"Oh, five or six years ago. She moved from the city, and when she came back she apparently found another doctor."

"So the sensible thing for me to do would be to find who her doctor is currently and to see what sort of medication he was prescribing for her, right?"

"That seems sensible to me."

But I knew who her current doctor was. And I also knew the vested interest he had in keeping Karen Lane his own. For the first time I started considering Dr. Glendon Evans a murder suspect.

"I really appreciate this, Doctor."

"Of course." A pause again. "Karen was a very striking woman."

"Yes, she was."

"I—" He stopped talking again and in his silence I could hear that he'd been smitten, too. "We went out a few times."

"I see."

"I'm afraid I was married and I'm afraid it got messy for everybody concerned."

This was the part where circumstances forced me to be a surrogate priest. I never much cared for the role. "I was afraid that if I went to the police with this, I'd get dragged into the papers myself and it would bring up some bad memories for my wife."

"I see."

"So if my name could be left out—"

"Of course."

"My wife and I have a much better marriage now." I made careful note of the fact that he didn't say "good marriage." Only "much better." His sadness got to me and I wanted to say the right soothing thing, but I didn't know what that would be.

"It was very good of you to call."

"I felt I owed it to Karen."

"Thank you, Doctor."

As I was hanging up, Donna appeared, leaning model-fashion against the doorjamb, imposing in a dark blue cashmere sweater, designer jeans, and short leather boots, her red hair wild as mountain water down her shoulders.

"Well, I guess I'm ready." She sounded like a little girl who was being sent off, much against her will, to a summer camp run by bona fide ogres.

"You ready?"

"I guess," she said. "But you're not." Then she smiled. "God, Dwyer, I really think we should start sort of a kitty so you can get yourself some new underwear and socks."

"Thanks."

"You're nearly forty-five."

"Gee, don't I like being reminded of that."

"And all your underwear and socks have holes in them. Like a kid."

"They're clean, though."

"That's true. They *are* clean. But—"

So I went over and grabbed her and yanked her back to the bed and she said, "I just got dressed."

And I said, "I think we should have some general underwear inspection here. I just want to make sure that you're not being hypocritical. How do I know *your* underwear isn't in rags?"

"Dwyer, you really are nuts, you know that?"

But she relented and let me inspect her underwear anyway.

19

"The name Sonny mean anything to you?"

"It's the name of a song."

"Yeah," I said.

"There was Sonny Liston."

"Right."

"And Sonny and Cher."

"Uh-huh."

"And Sonny James."

"Who?"

"Country-Western singer."

"Oh."

"Don't give me your crap about country-Western singers."

"All right."

It was one-thirty in the afternoon in Malley's Tavern on the Eighth Avenue side of the Highlands. The place smelled of beer, disinfectant, and peanuts. Strong warm sunlight brightened the aged wooden floor. Bob Malley, paunchy, bearded, wrapped around with the spotless white apron that is his pride, stood behind the bar he owned and idly flipped a quarter, checking heads or tails every time it came down. I imagine he does this as often as five hundred times a day. Some people find this the kind of minor social irritation that can turn nuns into psychopaths. But I'm used to it. Though he was a grade ahead of me, Malley and I have been friends since, respectively, first and second grade. I've seen him flip quarters probably twenty million times by now.

Ordinarily I come in three afternoons a week. Today I had two reasons to be there. To say hello and to ask for information. Malley remembers our school days with the reverence of Thornton Wilder recalling an autumn afternoon in New England.

"Sonny Tufts," I said.

"Oh. Yeah. Sonny Tufts. You want another shell?"

"Nah."

He grinned. "Donna's a good influence on you, Dwyer. You've cut your drinking in half since you met her. So when's the date?"

"We fornicate without benefit of clergy, Malley. We have no plans to get married. We're not ashamed. She's not even Catholic."

"That's my only reservation about her."

"Right."

"So what's with this Sonny jazz?"

I told him about the woman in the black leather and how she'd mentioned Sonny.

"And you were in Larry Price's house?"

"Yeah," I said.

"Then she probably meant Sonny Howard."

"Who?"

"Sonny Howard. Summer of our senior year. Remember we went to summer school so we could take a lighter load during the regular year?"

"Yeah."

"Well, he went to summer school, too. Except he hung around with Price and Forester and Haskins. Then he killed himself."

He tossed it away so casually it almost went right by me, like doing a bad double-take shtick. Then, "What?"

"He killed himself. Don't you remember? He jumped off Pierce Point."

"Give me another shell."

"I thought you didn't want one." He smiled and got me another shell.

"Tell me some more about him."

"Don't know much more about him," Malley said, setting down my beer.

"Why don't I remember him?"

"Probably tried to forget him."

"Why?"

"He sort of hung around Karen Lane. That's when you were chasing rich chicks and trying to forget all about her."

"He knew Karen Lane?"

"I don't think they were getting it on or anything—I mean, I don't think she put out very much when you came right down to it—but I remember toward the end of the summer they were together a lot."

"Why were people so sure he killed himself? I mean, Pierce Point, you could fall off real easy."

"There was a witness."

"Who?"

"You're being a cop again. Ease off, okay? I'm not especially fond of cops."

"So you've told me."

"Witness, I don't know, seems it was David Haskins."

"You're kidding?"

"You asked me. Why would I kid you?"

"David Haskins was the witness?"

"David Haskins was the witness."

I drained half my shell and set it down and watched white foam slide down into the yellow beer. I liked taverns, hearing the crack of cards as men played pinochle, and the clatter of pool and the sound of workingmen loud at the end of a workday. At four I used to sit in union taverns and eat salted hard-boiled eggs and sip my old man's beer and learn all the reasons why you should never trust Republicans.

"Killed himself," I said. "Killed himself."

"I take it you don't believe that."

I looked right at him and said, "No, Malley, I don't. Not in the least damn bit at all."

20 Mrs. Haskins was reluctant to tell me where her husband was employed. "If you're a friend of his, then you should know where he works," she said on the other end of the phone.

"I didn't say I was a friend, exactly, Mrs. Haskins. I said I was a classmate."

"Oh. I see. At the university?"

"No. High school."

"Oh."

"I really would like to speak with him."

"It's urgent or something?"

Years of police work had taught me that politeness is almost always more effective than belligerence. "I'm trying to locate someone, Mrs. Haskins. It's not a big deal, but I believe David could help me."

"You don't know him very well, do you?"

"Ma'm?"

"He's 'Dave.' He hates David. That's what his father always called him, and to be honest, he never cared much for his father."

"I see."

She sighed. "I suppose I sound terribly unfriendly, don't I?"

"Not at all. You're protective of your husband. That's an admirable trait."

"Yes, I suppose so, especially with the divorce rate these days." She paused and then said, as if with some effort, "He works at Smythe and Brothers. It's a bro- kerage downtown."

"Thank you, Mrs. Haskins."

"I just hope I've done the right thing."

"Thanks again."

I called Smythe and Brothers. An icy female voice told me that Mr. Haskins was out and would not be back until three-thirty. I thanked her, then phoned the tavern where Chuck Lane worked. He was out, too, I was informed, and wasn't expected back until probably six or so, when he started working. From him I'd wanted some more discussion on the subject of Karen's senior summer. Then I phoned Dr. Glendon Evans' of- fice and was told he was with a patient and would I mind sharing with her (that's what she said, the verbal equivalent of earth tones, sharing with her), but I just said no, I'd call back. I'd do my sharing alone.

I sat in the Toyota flush with the pull-up phone lis- tening to a radio report live from the Cubs training camp. Oh, it could be one hell of a year, the third-base coach allowed, that is, if the the X rays on their leading pitcher's arm came out okay, and if their best base stealer didn't take advantage of his free-agent potential and go play for the Dodgers, and if those unfortunate drug charges against their leading hitter got dropped. Oh, it could be one hell of a year.

I dropped in another quarter. The number I wanted was busy. I wasn't that far away. I decided, keeping the window down and the radio up, to drive out there, the summer-like seventy degrees making me feel younger than I had any right to.

This time there weren't any sheets blowing on the clothesline like sails on racing sloops. In fact, the small tract home looked battened down, garage door closed, curtains drawn. I parked in the drive and went up to the door and knocked and got exactly the response I'd figured on. Nothing.

I stood looking at the scruffy brown lawn and then at the endless row of similar houses stretching to the vanishing point. This was the step up from our fathers we'd been promised. All it showed was how far down our fathers had been in the first place. Uselessly, I knocked again.

Then the door opened abruptly and there stood Susan Roberts pretty as always. She wore a man's blue work shirt and jeans and her hair was pulled back in a soft chignon whose luster could be seen even in the shadows of the doorway. She had been crying, and very recently and very hard.

"Hello, Jack," she said.

"I'm sorry. I seem to have come at a bad time."

"No . . . it's just . . . you know, the thing with Karen and all."

"That's what I wanted to talk to you about."

She seemed surprised. "Karen?"

"If you wouldn't mind."

"Did something new happen?"

"I'm not sure."

She smiled a bit. "You always did like being mysterious. Come on in."

Five minutes later we sat at a Formica-topped kitchen table and looked out on a brown backyard and at the redwood veranda of the house on the opposite end of the backyard.

She had made us instant coffee in a small microwave. She set down gray pewter mugs and then sat down across from me. She sipped her coffee and I watched the beautiful life in her hazel eyes, the intelligence of them, the compassion of them. Then she said, "I'm just being selfish."

"How so?"

"I'm not really thinking of Karen. I mean, that's not why I was crying when you came to the door."

"Oh?"

"There's an old Irish saying that the person you really mourn at a funeral is yourself. That's what I was doing. Mourning myself." She had some more coffee and said, "Do you think about dying very often?"

"To the point of being morbid."

"Me, too." She sighed, knitted hands chafed from work but still long and beautiful in form. "Our kids are in high school. Gary still hasn't ever finished a novel. And every day I look in the mirror, I see this odd old lady taking my place there." She stared out the window again. "Karen wasn't so hard to understand, really. She just wanted to be young and beautiful forever." The lopsided smile again, the warm tears still on her perfect cheeks. "Is that too much for a woman to ask?"

I said, "Did you ever know her to hang around anybody named Sonny?"

"Sure. Sonny Howard."

"Right. Sonny Howard. Can you tell me anything about him?"

She narrowed her eyes. "Why bring up Sonny Howard after all these years?"

"It could be important."

"Why?"

"Maybe Karen didn't die of an accidental overdose after all."

"I knew it."

"You did."

"Sure." She snapped her fingers. "That's exactly what I told Gary."

"That she didn't kill herself?"

"Yes. She really didn't have it in her. I mean she tried that once and—"

"What?"

"Yes. Didn't you know that?"

"No."

"It was the summer she hung around with Sonny Howard, as a matter of fact."

"Did you ever know why?"

"Not exactly."

"She didn't give you any hint?"

"Just something happened. In July. I went away for a week's vacation with my folks. When I left she was fine. But when I came back she'd gotten into these terrible crying jags. I thought maybe it was over Sonny. She'd been hanging around him a few months, but then I remembered her telling me he was just a friend, so . . ." She sighed. "None of it ever made much sense to me."

"Do you ever remember her saying anything about Ted Forester or Larry Price or David Haskins?"

"Just that she was afraid of them."

"You mean physically?"

She shrugged. "I'm not sure. One time we were at a

123

party and they came in and she ran out the back door. Literally ran. But that was the strange thing, too."

"What was strange?"

"I can still remember their faces when they came in and saw her there at the party."

"What about it?"

"They looked just as afraid of her as she was of them."

"Where did Sonny fit in all this?"

"He hung around with Forester and the others. He was just here for summer school. Actually he went to St. Matthew's, but they didn't offer the courses he needed, so he came over here. He was just their friend, I guess."

"But she wasn't afraid of Sonny?"

"She never said so." She shook her head. "Doesn't it all seem so long ago, like some old movie?"

I finished my coffee. "I wonder if you'd do me a favor."

"Sure, Jack."

"Let me see the room downstairs where she stayed."

"Of course."

"Thanks."

The basement, like the rest of the house, was furnished in odds and ends, styles and colors that should have clashed, but that Susan's hand had brought together in an uneasy harmony. The basement was five degrees cooler than upstairs. It had red-and-white-tiled flooring, imitation knotty-pine walls, a low white ceiling. There was a furnace to the left, a small bathroom whose open door revealed sink-shower-stool, an overstuffed couch facing a massive relic of other days—a Buddha-like black-and-white 21-inch Motorola console—and finally a new but unpainted door that creaked back to show me a room with a severe little single bed, a bureau covered with expensive perfumes and bottles and jars and vials and vessels of makeup, and then a sturdy piece of rope used as a hanger for more clothes than most department stores would have to offer. The clothes—fawns and pinks and soft blues and yellows, silk and linen and organza and lamé and velvet—did not belong in the chill rough basement of a working-class family. There was a sense of violation here, a beast holding trapped a fragile beauty.

On the bed lay an old hardback copy of *Breakfast at Tiffany's*. I went over and picked it up, its burnt-orange cover bright even after all these years, the pen-and-ink sketch of Capote on the back just as calculated now as it was then. I opened the front cover: Karen Lane's name was written in perfect penmanship, but when I flipped to the back I saw that it was a library book checked out the last time on May 3, 1959.

Susan laughed. "I think it was the only book she ever read. She loved it. She'd never give it back."

"Really?"

"They'd send her notices all the time. Virtually threaten her. But she wanted to keep the copy she'd first read. No other copy would do. Finally, she just paid them for it and kept it."

"Mind if I take it?"

"Be my guest."

I looked around. "She was here one month?"

"Just about. But actually she'd been staying overnight here for the past six months." Her mouth tightened. "I suppose if I raise any question about Dr. Evans, I'll sound like a bigot."

"Not to me, you won't."

"Well, I met him twice at lunch with Karen. He has this very calm, polished exterior, but he also has a terrible temper. She came here several times with bruises he'd given her."

I planned to see Dr. Evans tonight. I was fascinated

by how easy it would be for a shrink to "accidentally" overdose somebody he lived with.

I studied the front of the book again, as if it were going to tell me something.

She said, "So did I miss anything the other night? I really wish I could have gone."

"You know how you feel about looking in the mirror and seeing this strange old lady there? That's how I felt at the reunion. We're getting to be geezers, Susan. Geezers."

She poked me on the arm girlishly and said, "Speak for yourself, Jack."

Then she walked me up and we exchanged a chaste kiss and I liked the hell out of her all over again the way I had back there in grade school.

21 The receptionist wore a gray suit with wide lapels and a frilly white blouse. Her nails appeared to be her pride, they were as red as manicuring and lacquering could make them. Perhaps they were compensation for the fact that she was one of those women who are almost attractive but not quite, a bit too fleshy, a bit too inexplicably sour, a bit too self-conscious that all the time you're watching her you're saying to yourself that she is not quite attractive. She gave the impression that clothes probably interested her more than people. She touched at long hair that had been carefully tipped with a color not unlike silver.

"David Haskins," I said, going up to her desk.

Smythe and Brothers occupied its own floor in a new and grotesquely designed downtown office building. It was all leather and wood and forest-green flocked wallpaper. It exuded the aura of a men's club where the average member is over age seventy-five.

"You have an appointment?"

She knew by looking at my blue windbreaker and open white button-down shirt and faded jeans that it was unlikely I had an appointment.

"I'm afraid I don't."

"May I ask what this is about?"

"Personal matter."

She assessed me once more. She was not impressed. "May I have your name, please?"

"Jack Dwyer."

She stood up. She was taller than I'd thought and her extras pounds were surprisingly attractive. But she wasn't any nicer. She pointed like a grumpy eighth-grade teacher to a leather couch the size of a life raft and said, "Would you take a seat, please?"

So I took a seat and proceeded to look through a stack of magazines, each reverential in different ways about the subject of money.

He came out fifteen minutes later and he didn't look so good. He didn't come all the way over to me. He sort of let her lead the way and he sort of stood behind her and peeked out around the padded shoulders of her jacket.

"Hello," he said, leaning out.

He was maybe five seven and twenty pounds over-weight and wearing one of those double-breasted suits only Adolphe Menjou could get away with. He was losing his auburn hair so fast you could almost hear the follicles falling off. He was also slick with sweat and gulping. He gulped, and I mean big comic gulps, as if he could not get enough air, every few seconds.

"Hello," I said.

"How may I help you?"

"Do you remember me?"

"Uh, sure."

"Jack Dwyer."

"Of course." He looked at the receptionist the way a very young boy looks at his mother. For help.

"I saw you at the reunion dance the other night, Dave."

"Right."

She said, "He's very busy."

He said, "She's right, Jack, I am." He gulped. "Very busy."

So I decided to jackpot. I wasn't going to get past his receptionist here if I didn't roll some dice. "I was wondering if you'd tell me why Ted Forester and Larry Price were pushing you into the car the other night."

"What?"

"You seemed to be having a fight with them. I wondered why."

This time his glance at the receptionist was desperate. This time he looked as if he were going to faint. "I don't know what you're talking about."

"Aw, Dave." I decided maybe a little folksiness would help.

"Please, Jack, I'm—"

"He's very busy," the receptionist said. She took him by the shoulders and turned him back in the direction of his office. The corridor was lined with stern black-and-white photographs of dour men who'd devoted their lives to money. They'd probably grown up reading Scrooge McDuck comic books and taking them literally.

Then she gave him a shove, as if pushing a boat out to sea on choppy waters.

"Nice to see you, Dave," I called after him.

She snapped her not unappealing body around and said, "Exactly what the hell do you think you're doing?"

"What I was supposed to be doing was talking to Dave Haskins. But you wouldn't let me."

"Get out of here."

"You must get paid a lot of money."

"You heard me."

"You like working around all this money?"

"*Get out.*"

I got out.

I didn't go far. I went down in the parking lot and found a drive-up phone where I could keep watch on the parking-ramp exit where I hoped Dave Haskins would be appearing soon.

I decided to call Dr. Glendon Evans. But first I prepared myself. I'd done *Cuckoo's Nest* in dinner theater, so I tried to get back in that character—I had played one of the garden-variety loonies—and I did a good-enough job that by the time I actually dialed his number, I sounded as if I were standing on a bridge and about to jump off. The nurse put me right through to Dr. Evans.

"Yes?" he said, concern tightening his deep voice.

"It's Dwyer."

"What?" He went from concern to anger. "I just stepped out of session because my nurse told me—"

"Forget what your nurse told you. You and I need to talk."

"I'm sorry for what happened to Karen."

"Not good enough."

"Exactly what does that mean, Mr. Dwyer?"

"It means that she died of an overdose of Librium."

"And so?"

"And so I'll bet you have a lot of Librium on hand."

"You're implying that I killed Karen?"

"It's a possibility."

"I loved Karen."

"That doesn't mean you wouldn't kill her."

"People don't ordinarily kill people they love, Mr. Dwyer."

"Of course they do. Spend a week in a squad car. You see it all the time."

"I didn't kill her."

"Did you ever treat Karen as a patient?"

"No."

"Be very careful here, Doctor."

"Are you threatening me?"

"Yes. Because if I think you're lying to me, I'm going to call the police and tell them I think I've put it all together. At the very least, the publicity won't do your practice a lot of good."

He sighed. "I'm not sure what you mean by 'treat.'"

"Psychoanalyzed her."

"That's an occupational hazard, Mr. Dwyer."

"Don't be coy, Doctor. You know what I mean."

A pause. "We were both lovers and friends, Mr. Dwyer. It was only natural that she tell me things about herself and her past."

"Did you ever give her any kind of medication that might loosen her inhibitions?"

"I don't know if I want to answer that question."

"I assume, then, that that means yes."

"I was trying to help her. As her friend."

What a powerful grip psychiatrists can have on people. Particularly people they might love. In the name of helping them, they can enslave them through deceit and manipulation and drugs forever.

"You knew you couldn't keep her otherwise, didn't you?"

"That's very damned insulting. Both professionally and personally."

"I'm going to be at your condo at six. I expect you to be there and I expect you to talk. I'm going to ask you some questions, and if I'm not happy with the answers, I'm going straight to the police."

I didn't say good-bye. I just hung up.

Two minutes later Dave Haskins came flying out of the parking ramp in a new blue Oldsmobile. Three minutes after that, I found a nice snug place ¼ quarter mile behind him on the expressway and decided to settle in and find out where he was taking us.

22 From bluffs of oak and birch you look down into a deep valley where the river runs wide and green and deep in the springtime. Every few years you see sandbag crews work around the clock to minimize the flood damage. During flood years the river itself becomes a political issue and has defeated at least two candidates in recent memory.

The marina was busy today. People were hammering, painting, scraping, washing boats of all sizes. Music from fifty radios clashed, and shouts loud as boyhood boasts floated on the soft air and then fell away like birds vanishing. Sunlight and water and sails caught the breeze. More than enough to make most reasonable people happy.

I parked up in the bluffs and got out, taking my binoculars with me. Haskins had pulled into the marina's private parking lot. Without a card to open the automatic device, I was never going to get in there.

I brought the 'nocs into focus and began following him from his car, down along the pier, past several clusters of chittering houseboat owners, to a small leg of pier where a splendid white yacht overwhelmed everything within sight.

Two men stood on the prow of the yacht. Ted Forester, tan, trim, silver-haired, wearing the sort of casual Western getup you associate with very rich Texans. And Larry Price, smoking one of those 100-mm cigarettes, blue windbreaker contrasting with his movie-star blond hair and his weary sneer. By age forty-three he had to be tired of hating people as much as he did. He had to.

It happened very quickly.

Dave Haskins had not quite gotten aboard when Larry Price reached out and slapped him. He hit him hard enough that Haskins fell back into Forester's arms. Then Forester grabbed Haskins and shoved him against the cabin. All this was in pantomime. It was not unlike a silent movie. Everything looked very broad and theatrical.

I had no idea what was happening here, but I felt certain it had something to do with a missing suitcase and with an accidental overdose that wasn't accidental at all and with the mysterious mission of a crazed woman on a black Honda motorcycle.

I got back in the Toyota and drove the rest of the way down the hills, swerving once to avoid a squirrel who sat by the roadside looking much cuter than any rodent had a right to, and then easing on into the traffic flow, flanked on one side by a BMW and on the other by a Porsche. These guys probably thought I was here to clean out some houseboat toilets that had gotten plugged up over the years.

I parked just outside the private gate. From the glove compartment I took the Smith & Wesson .38 I'd used back in my days on the force, pushed it down inside my belt, and then set off over the gravel to the yacht a quarter mile away.

The people I passed were as festive as carnival goers, smiling, laughing, saying hi though they didn't know me, standing atop houseboats watching speedboats cutting through the long miles of river lying east. There had been paddle wheelers here as recently as a hundred years ago, and now the smell of fish and the scent of mud and the white flash of birch made you want to be a boy of that era and see one of the big wheelers come sidling into the cove half a mile downriver.

When I got to the leg of the pier where the yacht sat, I touched the .38 as if for luck. They were below deck now, the vast white boat empty up top, its three red mast pennants flapping with the force of gunshots in the wind.

When I got abreast of the yacht, I moved quickly, jumping aboard without pause. Then I stood there, waiting to find out if they'd heard me. If they had, they'd come up through the small oak cabin doors. And they would not be happy.

From what I could see, the yacht had a large aft deck, an upper saloon and lounge, and carried decals that designated Twin Cummins main engines. There was a lower dining saloon, and it was there I assumed the three of them had gone.

Everything was given over to the wind here, the cold clear force of it, and the scent of water. I heard nothing from below.

Then a voice said, "You planning a party tonight?"

When I turned to him, I saw that he was a dapper elderly man in a Hawaiian shirt and white ducks and baby blue deck shoes. Liver spots like tattoos decorated his hairy white forearms. When he saw who I was he frowned, obviously disappointed.

"Oh, I thought you were one of the Forester party." His tone implied that I owed him an explanation for not being such.

Damn, I thought. My idea had been to get as close to the cabin as possible and hear what was going on. Standing here talking was bound to get them up from below deck. I wouldn't learn anything at all.

But then I got lucky.

A woman of similar age called to the man from down the dock. He waved to her.

"I'm with maintenance," I said quickly.

"Oh," he said, "maintenance." He said it as if he knew exactly what I was talking about. I was glad he did. Then, "My wife. She wants me to help her paint the walls. On our houseboat."

I wished he weren't talking so loudly. I wished he would leave.

She called again and he shrugged, as if embarrassed a woman would have such power over a man, and then he left.

I stood there counting minutes on my Timex again, waiting for them to burst through the cabin doors and demand to know what I was doing there.

Another three, four minutes went by. And nothing.

I touched my .38 for luck again, then crept over to the far side of the cabin and knelt down and pressed my ear very hard against the thin white wall.

I hoped the next few minutes would prove I would be well rewarded for all my trouble of the past hour or so.

23 I knelt to the left of two windows that looked down into the dining area. A single glimpse had shown me that Forester and Price stood over a chair in which Dave Haskins sat, hands in lap, head down, miserable.

Forester said, "There's one thing the three of us need to do. And that's keep calm."

"Calm, right," Price said. "With this little bastard thinking of going to the police."

In a voice that was almost a sob, Haskins said, "Larry, honest to God, I didn't say I was going to the police, I only said *maybe* we should."

"Maybe we should? You little candy-ass. Don't you know that would ruin us? Every goddamn one of us."

"Maybe they wouldn't prosecute," Haskins said. He sounded painfully young and naive.

"Right," Price said. "Maybe that fat-ass mayor of ours would give us a medal."

Forester said, "That's enough, Price."

A sullen silence ensued. There was the sound of wind, the aroma of meat cooking on a grill somewhere nearby, laughter warm as the sunlight.

Forester said, "I got another letter today. Just reminding us to be there tomorrow night at ten at Pierce Point."

Another silence. Once, Haskins moaned. Price swore continuously.

"I'll take care of this son of a bitch," Price said.

"You'll calm down and shut your mouth," Forester said. He had one those of those tempers you could push a long way but then suddenly no further.

"Two hundred thousand dollars," Price said. "We can't afford it."

"Do we have any choice?" Forester said.

"Oh yes," Price said. "I forgot all about your political ambitions. It'd be worth two hundred thousand to you to ensure that you got a shot at congress next time, wouldn't it?"

Haskins said, "We could go to the police. Tell them what happened. Tell them—"

Forester said, as if to a child, "Dave, try to understand something, will you?"

"All right, Ted."

"It's not so much a question of legal culpability here. It's a question of what would happen to our reputations once it got out. Think it through, Dave. Think of how your wife would feel, or your children, your friends at the office, the people you know at church. Think of how they'd look at you. In their eyes, you'd never be the same again. Every time they saw you, they'd think about it. They might not even mean to. But they would."

Another silence.

Dave Haskins said softly, "You're right, Ted. I wasn't thinking clearly."

"If that goddamn Dwyer hadn't come along the other night at the reunion, I would have beaten it out of her," Price said. "Who she was working with, I mean."

"You sure she was involved in this?" Haskins said. "Somehow—"

Price laughed. All his cynicism was in the sound. "Somehow you don't think she was the kind to get involved in shaking somebody down for money?"

136

"She wasn't cruel," Haskins said.

"No, she was the next thing to a saint."

"Be quiet," Forester said. "We have to decide what we're going to do about tomorrow night." He paused. "Does everybody have his share ready?"

"I do," Haskins said. He seemed like a good little boy doing just what the teacher wanted him to.

"I don't want to pay it," Price said.

"That wasn't what I asked you, Larry," Forester snapped. "I asked you if you had your share ready."

Price said, "Yes."

"Then please hand it over."

"What? Why to you?"

"Because I'm the one who'll take it tomorrow night."

"Bullshit."

"Then let's take it to a vote. All right?"

"A vote would be fine with me," Haskins said. He seemed to be in shock.

"All in favor of me taking the money, raise their hands."

"You bastard," Price said. "You know you can bully this little pecker around."

"Do you vote for me?" Forester said.

"Of course I do, Ted."

"Thank you, Dave."

"Assholes."

"I'd like your money," Forester said. "I'd like it now."

A pause. Then Price said, "I don't like this. I don't like this at all and I want to go on record as saying I don't like it."

The wind had come up and I was starting to lean in closer, maybe dangerously close, to the window when a voice floated over to me on the air currents.

"Say, are you sure you're with maintenance?"

It was my elderly friend. He was down on the pier. I

realized quickly enough that I probably appeared, kneeling down as I was, to be burglarizing the boat. He looked suspicious, angry.

He didn't give me time to respond, "Ted! Ted, are you down there! You'd better get up here!" he called.

I got to my feet, knees cracking and stiff from kneeling, and began hobbling across the deck.

Seeing me move toward him, he took the broom in his hand and held it crosswise, like a martial-arts weapon.

"I'm not going to hurt you," I said. "Just relax, all right?"

I jumped back on the pier, trying to get to my feet as I reached the wood.

Behind me, I heard Larry Price shout, "Hey! Stop!"

The old man put his broom toward me, but I just gently pushed it away. "Just relax and enjoy the day, all right? Don't get mixed up in this."

Price surprised me by doing a dash across the boat and clearing the water and landing on my back. He smelled of sweat and hair spray and heat. He was still strong in the sinewy way of high school days.

"Atta boy!" the old man shouted, as Price threw me to the pier.

Price got his arm around my neck and started to choke me. I hadn't been in this kind of street fight in thirty years. At first I had no idea what to do. He took my hair and slammed my head against the pier once. The old man said, "Kick his butt, Larry! Kick his butt!" And then Price did something foolish, he tried to turn my face toward his so he could hit me dead-on. I surprised him. I got him one clean shot with my elbow in the teeth, and it was enough to make him fall away, and for his open mouth to fill up immediately with thick red blood. I got to my feet and he started to get to his. I kicked him once very hard in the abdomen. He went over backward and sprawled on the pier.

"Hey, that's not fair!" the old man said. To him I was the Mad Russian in some goofy pro wrestling match.

Forester and Haskins were on the deck now and running toward me.

I took off down the pier, running as best I could given knees that were none too good to begin with.

The pier was still packed and it was easy to lose myself among the crowd and find my car and get out of there.

24 At the time we'd agreed to meet, Dr. Glendon Evans opened the door of his condo. I started across the threshold, the pines surrounding his aerie sweet on the dying day. Then I stopped. He had a gun, some kind of Mauser, and he wanted to make sure I saw it.

"Not exactly your style, is it?"

He wore an open white shirt and blue trousers with a brown leather belt and penny loafers without socks. He looked angry and he smelled faintly of bourbon. "I'm not going to take any of your shit, Mr. Dwyer. I'm warning you."

"You really think that's going to help?"

"I've done a little checking on you."

"I'm impressed."

"You used to be a cop."

"I would have been more than happy to tell you that myself."

"Cops have ways of getting people to confess to things they didn't do."

"And you're saying you didn't kill her."

"That's exactly what I'm saying."

"Then there's no reason for the gun."

"Does it make you nervous, Mr. Dwyer?"

"Of course it makes me nervous, Dr. Evans. You're an amateur. Amateurs terrify me."

He glanced down at the weapon in his hand as if it were a growth slowly eating its way up his arm. "I don't suppose I am very good at this sort of thing."

"No," I said, reaching out and gently taking the gun from his hand, "I don't suppose you are."

"I violated half the ethics I'm supposed to believe in."

"You want me to call you names?"

"Maybe I'd feel better if you did, Mr. Dwyer."

This was half an hour later. We sat in the breakfast nook. We were sipping some of his Wild Turkey again. The night sky was purple and starry. Jets rumbled in the gloom above like gods displeased.

"Tell me what happened."

"Drugs," he said. "I gave her drugs."

"How many times?"

"Twice."

I had some more whiskey and just stared at my fists.

"I—I thought it was the only way I could keep her." He shook his head as if it hurt to do so. "I'd never had to deal with anything like it before." He had some whiskey himself. "You know how I told you I rode around in Lincolns growing up?"

I nodded.

"Well, it was the same with women. Never any problem. My color rarely seemed to matter. I just naturally seemed to be attractive to women and I always took that for granted." More whiskey. A sigh half anger, half remorse. "I was a good lover. I know I was. I don't mean in bed necessarily, though even there I always tried to make sure that they had their satisfaction before I took mine." He waved a hand. "I mean I was a good lover in the sense that I tried to be as attentive and sensitive as possible. When things ended, it was always me who ended them, but even then I tried to make it as easy as possible. And it wasn't because I was bored, it was just—I knew there were more things I needed to learn from women. They're the great teachers, you know, women; the best ones are, at any rate."

I laughed. "It's true. But let's not let them know that."

He smiled. "I'm afraid some of them do." Then he went back to frowning. "I'd never had anybody treat me the way Karen did."

"As good and as bad."

"Exactly."

"But it's the bad things you remember, isn't it?"

"That's what's so odd. I know we must have had hundreds of good times—but now I can barely remember any of them."

I was just letting him talk, easing him into his confession. He was eager to give it and I was eager to hear it. We both just kind of had to be in the right emotional spot. I poured him more whiskey.

He said, "For two decades I've been telling men and women alike that the idea of sexual enslavement is largely a myth. Now I know better."

I said, "You must have been getting pretty desperate when you started with the Pentathol."

He surprised me by laughing. "In other words, you want me to tell you what I found out."

I shrugged. "There's no easy way to say this, Doctor, but it's not a case of you violating your ethics because you didn't have any ethics to begin with."

"I wish I could get indignant and argue with you."

"So what did you learn?"

"Nothing."

"What?"

"Contrary to popular belief, drugs don't always dislodge memories, at least not the kind I could give Karen without her being aware of them. If I could have strapped her down to an electro-shock table and given her Pentathol . . . but I had to do this on the sly, of course, over the course of long weekends up here."

"And you didn't find out anything at all?"

"I found out only one thing for sure." He hesitated.

"Yes?"

"The odd thing is, I still feel very protective of her. Even after all she put me through."

I poured more whiskey.

"Go ahead," I said.

"She may have killed somebody."

I did a double take Jackie Gleason would have been proud of.

He nodded. "The boy's name was Sonny Howard."

"Christ."

"Something happened the summer of her senior year. She had repressed it to the point that she couldn't talk about it even under the influence of the drugs. But she did begin talking about this Sonny Howard, and then she just broke down, sobbing and saying 'I killed Sonny, I killed Sonny' over and over again. I had to use a different drug to calm her down."

"You mind if I open this?"

"What's wrong?"

"I'm getting claustrophobic."

So I leaned over and opened the window and smelled the fresh pine and listened to birds and crickets and dogs. Evans started to say something, but I waved off his words.

"It getting to you?" he said after a time.

"You really think she could have killed somebody?"

He did not hesitate. "Yes."

"And you think she really might have killed Sonny Howard?"

"Yes."

"It would explain a lot, wouldn't it?"

"It would indeed, Mr. Dwyer. Her inability to make a commitment of any kind, her living in a sort of soap-opera fantasy world half the time, the sense she always gave you of somehow being afraid of virtually everything."

I closed my eyes and leaned my head back. I was beginning to realize there was one person I needed to talk to. The woman on the black Honda motorcycle.

"You're leaving?"

I was on my feet. I put out my hand.

"Are you going to report this?" he asked.

"Don't see any reason to."

"I'm a good doctor, Mr. Dwyer. Despite the way I behaved."

"I guess I'm going to have to take your word for that, aren't I?"

He tried to smile. It wasn't especially convincing. "Yes," he said, "yes, I guess you are."

25 The aerobics class was going on—women in expensive exercise suits doing boot-camp jumping jacks now—but the Honda was not in the parking lot to the left of the shopper.

The disco music was overpowering when I walked inside. I moved along the right-hand corridor, trying to keep my eyes from all the breasts and thighs and buttocks my gaze gravitated to so naturally. The women were as curious about me as I was about them. A few even smiled in my direction, not in the inviting way women do at private investigators in books, but just because this was a female domain and there was something vaguely naughty about my being there and that made them curious.

The west wall was all mirrors to make the place look bigger; the carpet was cheap indoor-outdoor stuff hopelessly worn; the stereo speakers could have sufficed at Yankee stadium. (At least the owners had great taste in music, the Crusaders working their assess off on a killer number called "Sometimes You Can Take It or Leave It," the pure unremitting jazz of it as exhilarating as any exercise you could do.) The place smelled of perfume and sweat. Lined up along the back were a rowing machine, a ballet bar, a stationary bicycle, and a Coke machine where, with two quarters, you could put back all the calories you'd worked off.

On the other side of a glass wall, a chunky woman with a bad red dye job and arms as thick as a fullback's sat working over books. Occasionally she poked a fat finger at a calculator so hard you wondered if she had something against it.

I knocked on the window. When she glanced up and saw me, she did not look happy.

I pantomimed Can I Come In, the music too loud for me to be heard otherwise.

She didn't pantomime. She just made a face.

I went over to the door and opened it up and went inside.

She said, "We don't get a lot of men here."

"So I see."

She picked up a package of Winston Lights, tamped one out, got it going, exhaled a long blue stream of smoke, and said, "So how can I help you?" She looked like Ethel Merman with a bad hangover. Her nametag said HI, I'M IRENE.

"There's a woman who works here."

The flesh around her eyes grew tight and her mouth got unpleasant again. "Yeah. So?"

"So she drives a black Honda motorcycle and so I'd like to know who she is."

"Why?"

"Is that really any of your business?"

"As a matter of fact, it is."

"Now why would that be?"

"Because she happens to be my best friend."

"I see."

"And I protect her."

"From my few experiences with her, I'd say she doesn't need a hell of a lot of protection."

She had some more cigarette. "She's high-strung."

"At least."

She glared at me. "What's that supposed to mean?"

"It means I think she's probably clinical."

She sighed. "She's had some problems, I'll admit. But now that her aunt's in the nursing home—" She allowed herself several cigarette hacks, then said, "Evelyn has spent some time in mental hospitals."

"I see."

"That doesn't mean she's crazy."

"No," I said and meant it. "No, it doesn't."

"Her aunt raised her; Evelyn's own mother died when she was six. And then there's what happened with Sonny. That's when all the trouble started."

"What trouble?"

She jammed out one cigarette in a round red metal ashtray and promptly lit another. "You want a Coke?"

"Sure. I'll get it for us. You want regular or Diet?"

Given her weight problem, I figured she'd say Diet Coke. For the first time she smiled. "You want to learn something today?"

"What?"

"There are reports that show that people who drink diet pop actually gain weight instead of lose it."

"So you want regular Coke."

"Right," she said, "regular."

So I went and got her a regular and me a Diet and could not help but look at least briefly at the wondrous backside of the little black woman conducting the class, and then I went back into the tiny office gray with smoke.

"So what's with her aunt?"

"Sonny dies," she said, slipping into present tense. "Her aunt doesn't believe anything the police say. She starts becoming obsessed."

"What did the police say?"

"Suicide."

"They said he jumped off Pierce Point?"

She looked surprised that I knew about Pierce Point. "Right."

"Was there a note found?"

"Suicide note?" Irene said.

"Right."

"No."

"Then why did the police assume it was suicide?"

She shrugged. "They said he was despondent."

"Did they say about what?"

"No. But they said they checked with his teachers and the teachers all said he was despondent. Even the aunt had to admit that. He was usually an A student. He went to summer school between his junior and senior year so he could graduate early. But then he screwed it up."

"Screwed up his grades?"

"Yeah. He got Ds. In summer school you have to get at least Cs."

"So how does Evelyn fit into all this?" Now I was talking in the present tense, too.

"Evelyn is five years younger, right, a very pretty but very high-strung kid. Always had problems. Manic depression, actually. Well, when Sonny buys it, the aunt puts everything on Evelyn. She expects Evelyn not only to share the grief but to spend the rest of her life with her, too. The aunt has money, right, so the aunt builds Evelyn her own wing on the house and Evelyn is expected to stay there the rest of her life, right, and to get caught up in all her obsessions—her hypochondria (this woman has sent a dozen doctors screaming into the sunset), her paranoia about her investments (I mean most of the stockbrokers in this town would rather have gasoline enemas than deal with her), and with proving that Sonny was actually pushed off Pierce Point by persons unknown. So Evelyn, being none too stable herself, does in fact get caught up in all this. Very caught up. And in the process becomes sort of a half-ass detective, really going into Sonny's life and particularly into Sonny's life the summer between his junior and senior year." She stopped.

"And?"

"And to be honest, I don't know so much about lately."

"Lately?"

"The past few weeks."

"You haven't seen her?"

"Oh, I see her. But she's in one of her—moods." Her voice was an odd mixture of anger and sorrow. I liked her. She was tough in the way good people are tough. "I mean, I don't think we've split up or anything. She just gets—"

"Kind of crazy."

"Yeah, I guess it wouldn't be unfair to put it that way. Kind of crazy."

I thought of how she'd said 'split up.' Obviously she wanted me to know they were lovers.

"I wonder if you'd give me her address."

"You gotta know I'm going to ask you why?"

"Because I may be able to help her."

"True blue?"

"True blue. I may have a lead of sorts on Sonny."

"Everything's in her aunt's name."

"Huh?"

"House, credit cards, even her Honda."

"I see."

"Just look up her aunt's name in the phone book and you'll have the address."

"Thanks."

"She was supposed to be here tonight but she didn't show up. Didn't phone or anything. That's why I had to pull Mimsy in."

Now I wanted to leave and she still wanted to talk. She said, "I guess there's one thing I should tell you."

"What's that?"

"She can get kind of violent."

I thought of what she'd done to Donna and to Glendon Evans. Not to mention me. I said, "Yeah, I've heard rumors to that effect."

"But even if she did hurt you, she wouldn't mean to."

I smiled. "I'm sure that would make me feel a lot better."

She laughed and went into another cigarette hack and said, "She's great at apologies. I guess that's what

I'm really trying to say. She does these terrible things—anybody else I would have left years ago—but she's got this fantastic way of apologizing. You ever know anybody like that?"

In fact, I had.

Her name had been Karen Lane.

I thanked Irene and left.

26 I called American Security to see if they'd need me tonight (supposedly we work four nights on, three off, like firemen in some cities). They didn't. Next I called Donna, told her about my last three conversations.

"So this Sonny Howard was a friend of Forester and Price and Haskins and you think there's a possibility that Karen Lane killed him."

"A few people seem to think so."

"But why would she have killed him?"

"That's why I'm going to look up Evelyn."

"Then who killed Karen Lane?"

"If I knew, I'd call Edelman."

She sighed. "Boy, Dwyer."

"Come on."

"What?"

"You're trying to make me feel guilty about not taking you along."

"Am I succeeding?"

"No, because Evelyn is somewhere on the loose and she's not quite hinged properly."

"So I noticed."

"So what are you and Joanna doing?"

"Well, *Bringing Up Baby* is on PBS, so I guess we're going to watch that."

"You don't like Katharine Hepburn."

"I just can't get past all her mannerisms."

"Then concentrate on Cary Grant."

"I'd rather concentrate on you."

"You can't go."

"Boy, that's pretty cynical, Dwyer. Thinking I'd only compare you to Cary Grant because I wanted to go along."

"Right."

"It's a good thing I'm not sensitive."

"Bye, hon."

"Please, can't I?"

"Bye."

"Please?"

The three-story gabled house sat on a shelf of land dense with elm, maple, and spruce. A gravel road led up to it. A ring-necked pheasant ambled in front of my headlights and gave me a dirty look. I hit the brakes, the Toyota nearly doing a wheelie. The pheasant did not seem impressed. He didn't speed up at all. He just continued walking his way across the gravel drive and into the night.

I sat there, B.B. King loud suddenly on the FM jazz station I was tuned to, wailing very lonely there on the spring night, a night cold enough for a winter coat. I was still mad at the pheasant, or whatever feeling is supposed to be appropriate to a pheasant who has pissed you off (I guess I wanted to have a talk with him about traffic safety, you know—about looking both directions before you cross any thoroughfare, gravel drives included), and it was while I sat there kind of scanning the underbrush in the wash of my headlights that I saw the black glint.

At first it registered as nothing more ominous than something black and something metal and something shiny glimpsed through the dead brown spring weeds.

But after a few seconds I knew what it would be. What it was.

A black Honda motorcycle.

I clicked off the radio and suddenly the night silence was a roar of distant dogs and trains.

I got out, but at first I didn't go anywhere. I took a piece of Doublemint out of my pocket and folded it over and put it in my mouth and I stared up at the big house. It was exactly the kind of place my old man always had dreamed of, here on several acres of its own land, enough maybe to plant some corn and tomatoes and carrots and green beans on a plot in the back to convince yourself you were really still a farmer the way all the Dwyers only two generations ago had been, and say "screw it" to all the burdens of city life. But watching the house now, I recalled how it hadn't worked out for him, not at all, how he'd ended up owing $700 on a six-year-old Pontiac whose transmission had never worked right, and how the closest he ever came to the country was the cemetery where he got planted.

I heard a moan.

I had put it off as long as I could, and now I couldn't put it off any longer. I had to go over there and see what I'd find. This had happened to me a few times on the force, when I'd let somebody else have first peek at somebody badly injured or dead. But now first peek belonged to me.

When I saw her I thought again of Karen and how she'd looked there at the last in my arms and I thought of my father there in his hospital bed and I thought of a wino I'd seen beaten by a couple teenagers, I just

151

remembered the eyes and the fear that gave way to a curious kind of peace, some secret they knew just before pushing off, some secret you only got to understand when you were once and for all *going* to push off.

I knelt down next to her there in the weeds. She wore, as always, her leathers. Now the torso part was sticky with red. Somebody had shot her in the chest. The blood was like a bad kitchen spill, splotchy and gooey. It was warm and smelled. I got my hand under her blond hair the color and texture of straw. Her blue eyes watched me all this time. The fear was giving way, fast. In a couple of minutes she was going to know the secret everybody from St. Thomas Aquinas to Howard Hughes had wanted to know.

"Evelyn, I need you to answer one question."

Just watching me.

"You've been following Karen, trying to get some proof that she killed Sonny."

Faintly, a nod.

"Did you kill Karen?"

Shaking her head. Then blood began bubbling in the corner of her mouth. I closed my eyes.

Then she cried out, "Sonny!" And now it was my turn to watch her, watch the secret come into her eyes, and feel her start to go easy in my grasp.

I said an "Our Father" for her, not knowing exactly what else to do, just an "Our Father" silent to myself, as a train rattled through the night in the pass above, and a dog barked at a passing car somewhere down the road.

I checked her neck, her wrist, and then put my head to that part of her chest not soaked in blood. She had pushed off, no doubt about it. I took her hand and stared at her face there, lit by my flashlight, at the freckles, the forlorn mouth; and for the first time I was curious about her—what her favorite foods had been, what sort of music she'd liked, what her laugh might have sounded like on a summer afternoon. There is an Indian sect that believes you can see a person's soul leaving the body if you watch out of the corner of your eye. I watched out of the corner of my eye, but I didn't see anything. Maybe it was gone already; or maybe it was just waiting for me to leave before it rose, shimmering and transcendent; or maybe, the worst thought of all, there is no soul—maybe the body I stared down at was no different from the body of a rabbit or cat you saw on a dusty roadside, filthy in death and useful only to those who relish the taste of carrion. Maybe that was the secret, and if it was, I didn't want to know. I didn't want to know it at all.

I turned out my light and left her there in the weeds and went on up the sloping gravel drive to the dark house.

I tried my American Express card and when that didn't work I went over into the garage and got a screwdriver and tried that and that didn't work either, so I did what the real novice criminal does; I took off my jacket and wrapped it around my fist and then pushed my fist through the back-door window, the noise of smashing glass almost obscene in the stillness, and then I took the jacket off my hand and slid it back over my body and simply reached in through the broken window and undid the lock.

Inside, I went through a back porch that smelled of apple cider and lawn fertilizer. Then I went through a kitchen that smelled of the sort of food you fix in a wok. Then I went through a dining room big enough to give a major restaurant some problems. Moonlight shone softly through a line of long, narrow windows onto the ghostly white cloth covering the formal dining table and the built-in buffet. The living room had a soaring ceiling, a real Palladian window, and a fireplace above which hung a McKnight print. Evelyn may have suffered from mental problems; she certainly hadn't suffered from poverty.

I went up the stairs to my right, the sound of my footsteps lost in the deep-pile carpeting and the noise of the wind outside.

The second floor was every bit as impressive as the first. There was a master bedroom Tut would have envied, complete with a sunken bathtub big enough to hold swim tryouts in, and a den filled with forty years of Book-of-the-Month-Club selections, all those oddments from curios like Jack Paar to the real stuff like William Faulkner.

The room where the boy had lived was easy enough to identify. There were a single bed, a bookcase with twenty-five cent paperbacks of Robert Heinlein, Jerry Sohl, Mickey Spillane, and several of the Dobie Gillis books. The closet contained chinos with little belt buckles in back, the kind that had been popular at the time he'd died in 1962, and the bureau drawers orderly stacks of white socks and jockey shorts. On the walls were posters of the Beach Boys (Brian looked to weigh about 100 pounds in those days) and Elvis with his sneer.

In other words, nothing useful.

Two doors down the hall my luck changed. What appeared to be nothing more than Evelyn's room with its Wedgwood blue curtains and matching bedspread and stuffed animals (a duck's eyes seemed to sparkle with intelligence, watching me) proved otherwise once I sat down at her desk.

Next to a Wang computer was a large reel-to-reel tape recorder that was patched into a phone system sitting next to it. I wondered what this was all about. I turned on the recorder, tiny amber lights haunting the darkness, and sat down and listened.

"You know who this is, don't you?" This was Evelyn's voice.

"I'm getting very goddamn tired of this."

"You're protecting that woman. It's time you came forward."

"I have to go now." Not until then had I realized whose voice it was. Ted Forester's.

"If you go, I'll phone the police."

A sigh. "How much money do you want?"

"You should know me better than that by now, Mr. Forester."

"I—I'm in no position to go to the police."

"You know she killed him."

"I really need to—"

"Why are you protecting her?" Anger had begun to edge into her voice.

"I'm not protecting her."

"Of course you are. All three of you are. And I won't let you anymore. I won't let you. You'll see." By now she was in tears, her own kind of dark psych-ward tears. There was rage but there was no power, she was drifting off into her madness and so she did the only thing she could. She hung up.

I let the tape roll and sat there in her room and felt sorry for her again, thinking of her freckles and her crazed eyes. She was one of those born truly luckless; not even money could put her life back together again.

The next conversation was with Larry Price. Predictably, he was not as diplomatic as Forester had been. He cursed her a lot and threatened her a lot and it was he, not she, who hung up.

Then came Dave Haskins. From the beginning, he sounded miserable. Over and over he said, "You don't understand what's going on here. We're not—" Then he stopped.

"You're not what?"

"I—I can't say. Ted and Larry would—"

"Hurt you?"

"Yes, God, don't you understand that? That's exactly what they'd do. They'd hurt me."

"She killed Sonny. And I'm taping all these conversations to turn over to the police. And—"

"If you want to talk to somebody, don't talk to me, all right? Ted and Larry are the ones—"

"I followed you the other day."

"What?"

"I followed you."

"Why?"

"I follow all of you. I follow everybody." She paused. "You almost went to the police, didn't you?"

He said nothing.

"Didn't you?"

Very softly: "Yes."

"You're getting tired of it, aren't you?"

"Yes."

"You're the only good one of the three. And I'm not just saying that. I've followed all of you and I've talked to you on the phone and I know that you're the only good one of the three. I know that." She was going off again, and the rest of the conversation consisted mostly of her telling him how good he was and wouldn't he please go to the police. But all he said at the end, and obviously without any conviction, was "Give me a few days to think about it, all right? Please give me a few more days."

The next call was the real shocker and as soon as I heard who it was I thought of what Dr. Evans had said, that Karen's pattern was to have a new lover waiting in the wings before she got rid of the old one. And Evans had sensed that there was, in fact, a man in her life at the time Karen had been withdrawing from him.

I sat there in the prim pleasantness of the dead woman's bedroom and listened to the voice, an old-familiar voice, and didn't know what to think or say or do; I just thought of all the people involved, and all the people betrayed.

After a time, I turned off the player and just sat there, listening to the night wind and lonely creaking of a house where anything like real life had stopped in the summer of 1962.

Then I got angry and it was what I needed just then, real anger, and I went down the stairs and out of the house and down the gravel road past where Evelyn lay sprawled in her leathers like some piece of trendy violent sculpture, and I got in my Toyota.

Ten minutes later I was at a drive-up phone.

"You can go home now."

"Really?" Donna said. "You're not worried about that woman anymore?"

"She's dead."

Pause. "You don't sound so good, Dwyer."

"I don't feel so good."

"Why don't you meet me at my apartment in an hour or so."

"There's something I've got to do."

"It doesn't sound like something that's going to make you very happy."

So I thought about it and then I talked about it and then I felt much better than I should have, much better than I would have keeping silent. Donna does that for me.

27 "Jack."

"Hi. Gary home?" I tried sounding as if it were Christmas and I were dropping off presents for the kids and I were wearing a red Santa cap and a glow from toddies, but I knew better and she knew better, too.

"What's wrong?"

"Nothing."

"Jack, come on. I've known you a long time. Something's up."

"It's probably nothing. I just need to see Gary."

"He's at school."

"At this time?"

"He teaches a course in creative writing at night. Adult ed."

"I see." I stared past her into the house. It was inevitably tidy, tidy as she was, with the same kind of poor but resolute dignity. "I'm going to ask you something, and I wouldn't blame you if you'd ask me to leave."

"God, Jack." She put her hands to her face. "You're scaring me."

"I'm sorry."

"Oh, Jack."

And then she came up to me and slid her arms around me and I held her, sexless as a sibling in the soiled light of her living room there, and I permitted myself only certain pleasures in her embrace, the clean smell of her hair, the faintest shape of her small breasts against my chest, the ageless sense of the maternal that bound me up when I finally relaxed and let her begin stroking the back of my head. I was the one who had frightened her, yet she was calming me down. I thought of Glendon Evans' remark that women were the great teachers. And so they were.

"Mom?"

The boy's word said many things, all of them shocked, all of them scared.

She eased away from me and said, "It's just Jack, honey. He's just—sort of upset about something. Jack, I don't believe you've met Gary Junior."

"No," I said, trying to find my voice like a freshman who's been caught kissing a girl in the sudden presence of her father. "No, I haven't."

So I made a big beer-commercial thing of shaking the kid's hand and cuffing him on the shoulder and standing back as if he were a car and I were appraising him and I said, "He's got your looks, Susan." He was a chunky kid with his old man's shaggy brown hair and that odd gaze of belligerent intelligence, as if he knew something vital but would be damned if he ever told you what it was.

She smiled. "And Gary's brains."

He was seventeen or so and he just wanted out of there. "Can I take the Pontiac?"

"I just finish telling you how smart he is and he says 'Can I take the Pontiac?' Honey, it's 'May I take the Pontiac?'"

"May I, then?"

"You know where the keys are. And tell Jack that you were glad to meet him."

But I was the guy he'd just seen in some kind of curious embrace with his mother and he didn't feel much like saying that he was glad he'd met me. And I didn't blame him at all.

After he was gone, she looked at me levelly and said, "You were going to ask me something that might cause me to ask you to leave."

"Right."

"Well."

"Does Gary have a writing room?"

"As a matter of fact, he does. The attic."

"I wonder if I could see it."

"You want to see Gary's writing room?" For the first time irritation could be heard in her tone. "Why?"

"It's not anything I can explain."

"Jack, please tell me what's going on. I don't want to be angry with you. I don't want to ask you to leave, but I need you to tell me the truth."

I thought about that, about telling her the truth, but it would be too complicated and would only hurt her more. And at this point, I wasn't sure of what the truth was exactly, anyway.

I said, "I think Karen gave him something."

"Karen?"

"Yes."

"Gave him what?"

"I'm not sure."

"Jack, this is all so crazy."

"She may have given him something that will shed some light on her death."

"Well, you don't think Gary had anything to do with it, do you?"

I said it very quickly. "No."

She sighed and broke out in a grin that was accompanied by tears of relief. This time she hugged me hard enough to hurt my back.

"You had me so scared," she said. "I didn't know what was going on." Then she took my hand and said, "I'm going to take you to the steps leading to the attic now, Jack, and you take all the time you want."

*   *   *

It was about what you might expect, an unfinished attic filled with bookcases containing hundreds of paperbacks, everything from Thomas Mann to Leonard Cohen, from e.e. cummings to Gregory Corso.

What I wanted I found with almost no difficulty. I only had to rattle open and rifle through a few file drawers, jerk back and sort through a few desk drawers.

And there it was.

I slid it inside my shirt and went back downstairs.

She must have heard me coming down the steps because she called from the kitchen, "Come on out here."

When I got there, she said, "You know what I made tonight? Gingersnaps. Real ones. Here. Have one."

So I had one and then I had two and all the while we made quick talk of weather and gingersnaps and teen-agers these days, and then she said, "Well, find anything?"

"'fraid not."

"Oh, I'm sorry, Jack."

"It's all right."

She said, "You want another one?"

"No, thanks." I had my hand on the back door. I wondered if she knew. The thing I'd shoved down inside my shirt seemed to be glowing. She had to see. Had to know.

"You sure?"

"I'm sure."

She laughed. "Well, I hope the next time I see you, it's on a happier note."

"It will be, Susan. It will be."

Then I was gone.

28 Wilson had been built during the final economic boom of the sixties, when so many dead young Americans over in Nam meant so many live jobs over here, and it had been designed, by an architect who was too tricky by half, with a waterfall between the two main sections of the rambling two-story brick structure, a comic imitation of Frank Lloyd Wright.

It was nearly ten-thirty and people were drifting out to their cars in the lot. They were middle-aged with middle-aged flesh and an air of middle-aged dreams. At forty you don't take night-school courses because you've got an eye on glory; all you've got an eye on is the next rung up in some vast drab institution somewhere. Level Six, as the people in Personnel might say, the exception being classes such as Creative Writing, where glory is still possible, even if said glory does only come in the form of a fifteen-dollar check for your first professional sale to a magazine promoting the likelihood of an imminent alien invasion or the possibility that Liberace has joined James Dean and John Kennedy on an island in the Pacific known only to an ancient race of henna-skinned religious cannibals.

The inside of the high school was almost lurid with fluorescent light and the odor of cleaning solvent. The main hall was jammed with people heading for cars. I asked one of them for directions to Mr. Roberts' room and she told me.

When I got there, he was sitting on the edge of his

desk, smoking a cigarette and talking earnestly to a plump woman in a yellow pantsuit that had gone out of style with Jimmy Carter. She was smoking, too.

Watching him, I had the sense that he must be a good teacher, taking everybody just as seriously as he took himself, looking for the same talent in his students he sought in himself, and probably finding it in neither.

He stuck out a Diet Pepsi can for the woman to push her cigarette in and then he said, "All you need to remember, Mary, is that it's better to put in the things about your childhood later on, after you've got the reader hooked on the story line itself. I'd start out right off with the ambulance scene. It's really gripping."

The way she smiled, she might just have discovered the real meaning of life.

"Oh, Gary," she said, "I just love taking your class."

"You're doing very well, Mary. Very well."

She pulled a purse big enough to hold a Japanese car over her wide shoulder, picked up a pile of schoolbooks, nodded good-bye, and left the room. On her way out, she saw me and smiled. "He's wonderful, isn't he?" And he was—patient, caring, taking pleasure in her pleasure.

I smiled at her and her enthusiasm. She was my age maybe, and she radiated a high, uncomplicated passion for life. And that's something I've always only been able to envy, that kind of simple and beautiful enthusiasm for things. I'm always too busy worrying about what can go wrong or wondering what the guy *really* meant.

Gary still hadn't seen me. He was busy pushing papers and books into a briefcase as scuffed as his shoes always were. I watched him there amid all the empty desks, like lifeboats on a mean vast ocean, his graying hair pulled back into a ponytail, his jeans still bell-bottomed, his eyeglasses rimless. He was the last of the species *hippie*. At his funeral somebody would probably read something from one of the Doors' songs.

I said, "How long were you having an affair with Karen, Gary?"

He didn't look up. He knew exactly what had been said and he knew exactly who'd said it.

I came into the room. He still hadn't looked up.

I put the manuscript on the desk. The room was painted the dull green of most institutions. It seemed to hush us with its terrible powers to disintegrate personalities. Finally, I said, "I didn't get a chance to read it all. But I read enough of it."

All he said was, "Susan know about this?"

"No."

"Jesus," he said. "I really have fucked things up, haven't I?"

"Yeah, I guess you have."

"The only other time I was unfaithful was back in the sixties. At some kind of English teachers' seminar. This woman with a face that reminded me of Cherie Conners. You remember Cherie Conners?"

"Sure."

"I always wanted to screw her. That's sort of what I was doing with this woman at the English teachers' convention. Closing my eyes and pretending she was Cherie. You know she died of an aneurysm a few years ago? Cherie, I mean?"

"I heard that. She was a nice woman."

"It's all crazy bullshit, isn't it, Dwyer?"

"Yeah, it is."

"You going to tell Susan?"

I kept staring at him. He was treating this as if I'd caught him in nothing more than a simple case of adul-

164

tery. But Karen had been murdered, and so, earlier tonight, had a sad woman named Evelyn.

"What time did your class start?"

"Eight o'clock."

"Little late for night school, isn't it?"

"We took a vote the first night of class. Everybody wanted eight o'clock." He took out his cigarettes. Lit one. "You gave 'em up, huh?"

"Yeah, almost."

He coughed, as if for emphasis. "Wish I could."

"You know a woman named Evelyn Dain?"

For the first time I could see that he was lying. He just sort of shrugged.

"She was killed tonight. Murdered."

"I'm sorry to hear about that. She a friend of yours?"

"She was obsessed with the idea that Karen Lane killed a boy named Sonny Howard. This was the summer we were going into senior year."

He talked with smoke coming out of his mouth. "Well, that's bullshit."

I picked up the twenty-page manuscript. It was sloppily typed, with many strikeovers, many words written in the margins with pencil. *The Autumn Dead.* It's about Karen, isn't it?"

"In ways. It's my version of Holly Golightly, too. Very selfish but very fetching. A woman you need to get rid of but can't. She had a story of her own, her own *True Life Tale,* as she called it. She said we could turn it into a good novel if we collaborated. She said all it needed was a good second draft. She never got around to showing it to me, though."

"Karen tell you everything that happened to her?"

"She told me some of the things."

"Such as?"

"Oh, about her brother. Things like that."

"What about her brother?"

"He's kind of a bastard. She's always tried to help him but it hasn't helped much."

"She ever mention anything about blackmailing anybody?"

He laughed. "God, Dwyer, being a cop really screwed up your mind, didn't it? We're talking about Karen Lane here. She was a cheerleader, she liked to go shopping, she got very sentimental over Barry Manilow records—" He shook his ponytail, trying to rid his eyes of tears. They were big and silver, the way his wife's had been earlier.

I didn't say anything for a time.

He turned away from me and sometimes he snuffled and sometimes he smoked but mostly he just kept shaking his head, his ponytail bobbing, as if to awaken himself from a terrible dream.

I said, softly, "It started when she moved in, you and her, I mean?"

"No. A few months before."

"How'd you keep it from Susan?"

"We just sneaked around a lot. Motels, I guess. Karen had credit cards." He turned back to me. "I knew she was keeping something from me."

"Any idea what it was?"

"No. It was—almost as if it was the central part of her personality. You know, like missing the one vital clue in a mystery. If you knew what she was holding back, then you could understand her. But . . ." He shrugged. "She had nightmares a lot."

"She ever talk much about Ted Forester or Larry Price or Dave Haskins?"

"Price came to see her one night."

"What?"

"Yes. He came to the door and asked if she would come out to the car with him."

166

"She went?"

He nodded. "When she came back, I could see a welt on her cheek. As if he'd slapped her."

I said, "Was this about the time you started hearing from Evelyn?"

This time he sighed, acknowledged he knew her. "Yes. She started calling me and said she wanted me to help her prove that Karen had killed a boy named Sonny Howard. She scared me, this Evelyn. Really a crazy woman."

"You didn't go to the reunion?"

"No, I didn't. Why?"

"Curious."

"Jesus, you think I had something to do with Karen's death?"

"Possibly."

"Christ, Dwyer."

I touched the manuscript again. The parts I'd read detailed how a middle-aged man falls miserably in love with a beautiful woman from his past and pleads with her to run away with him. "You were in love with her."

"Yes. In a very positive way." He exhaled blue smoke. "We were going to go away together."

He said it so easily, so confidently, that it wasn't half as funny as it should have been. She'd been with many men, good and bad, but they'd had one thing in common, and that was the power of their money to protect her from her demons. She and Gary Roberts would have lasted maybe three months.

"You don't believe me?"

"I believe you," I said.

"I gave Karen things nobody else ever had."

"Tell me more about Larry Price."

"What about him?"

"He ever come around again?"

"No. But he called."

"When?"

"A few weeks after he came over. She was very upset, sobbing, when she hung up. Then she went out to see her brother."

"She didn't say why?"

"No."

"I need to say something here and I'm going to come off sanctimonious," I said.

He looked at me with his middle-aged eyes and said, "I know."

"You've got a fine wife."

He nodded. "Don't you think I feel like shit?" Then, "So you're not going to tell her?"

"Of course not."

"Thanks."

"You can still patch it up."

"I want to. It's just—" He shrugged. "It was like being a teenager again. It really was. I mean, we made love everywhere possible. Wrote notes—" His laugh was sour. "While all the time Susan was at home being a good wife."

I set my hand on his shoulder and thought of us as young boys playing ball one summer, and how I could never have predicted that thirty-five years later we'd be standing here having this conversation. We were part of the same generation, falling away now, some of us, to be joined later by the rest of us, our moment on the planet vanished, the sunlight on baseball grass shining for different generations.

I felt sorry for him and angry with him and even half-afraid for him, a marriage being not so easy to put back together again, and at last I said, "You're a goddamn good teacher, you know that?"

"Really?"

"Yeah. I stood in the doorway watching you with that last woman. You're really good."

"Well, thanks. I mean, I'm not sure I'm ever going to sell anything as a writer. But as a teacher—"

I said, "Why don't you go home and take her out somewhere nice."

"Tonight?"

"Hell, yes, tonight."

"Why will I tell her we're going?"

"Tell her because you just realized all over again how much you love her."

He laughed. "You should write sappy greeting cards, Dwyer. That's a great idea."

"Nobody's ever accused me of that before."

"What?"

"Having great ideas."

29 "So who has the suitcase and what's in it?"

"That's the trouble."

"What?"

"I don't know."

We had been in bed for close to an hour now. My shoes were off but that was it. Donna was in her blue thigh-length football jersey with the big 00 on the front. She looked attractively mussed and I wondered what she saw in me anyway.

"You want a back rub?" she said.

"No, thanks."

"You want some underwear inspection?"

"I wish I did."

"You want some herbal tea?"

"Sorry."

"You going to let me help you?"

"I guess not."

"Is it okay if I turn on the tube then?"

"Sure."

"Will you at least take off your clothes?"

So I got out of my clothes and got under the fancy blue-and-white gridwork comforter and tried to watch David Letterman.

"He's such an ass," Donna said.

"I know. So why are we watching him?"

"Nothing else on."

"You pay fifty-one dollars a month so you can have thirty-eight cable channels and you say there's nothing else on?"

"You want to argue? Will that make you feel better?"

"Apparently."

"All right," she said. She picked up the remote deal and clicked off Letterman and then sat up Indian-legged with her container of Dannon banana yogurt in one hand and her handful of raisins in the other. A white plastic Dairy Queen spoon stuck out of the Dannon. She always kept her Dairy Queen spoons and she went to the Dairy Queen a lot. "All right," she said.

"All right what?"

"All right your face is sort of messed up from somebody hitting you. And all right your high-school girlfriend is dead, presumably murdered. And all right a crazy, sad woman named Evelyn got blown over her motorcycle by somebody probably equally crazy. So, all right, start talking."

"About what?"

"About how you're feeling."

"I'm feeling like shit."

"So tell me about feeling like shit, Dwyer. Tell me all about it because I can't stand it when you get quiet like this. You just sit there and suffer and it's terrible. For both of us."

"I feel like shit is all. Doesn't that sort of say it?"

"Are you feeling like shit because maybe you sort of got a crush on Karen Lane again?"

"I knew that's what you were thinking. And the answer is no."

"Are you feeling like shit because you don't know what's in the suitcase?"

"Partly."

"What are you guessing is in the suitcase?"

"Something that will explain what really happened to Sonny Howard and will also explain why Forester and Price and Haskins are willing to pay so much for it."

"And who are you guessing has the suitcase?"

"That I don't know yet. That's why I'm going to the park—" I glanced at my Timex. It was well after midnight. "Tonight."

She dropped some raisins into her yogurt and said, "You're kind of menopausal, you know that? I mean the way you deal with things."

"Gee, thanks."

"No. You really are. You kind of go through these hot flashes and do irrational things."

"Such as what?"

"Such as going to the park."

"That's irrational?"

"Of course it is. That's the kind of thing you should call Edelman about. If there's going to be an exchange of the suitcase for money, then the police should be there, not you."

"This is different."

"No, it's not. It's menopausal."

She clicked David Letterman back on. He was being coy as usual because the topic was sex, a subject he seemed to find disgusting.

I lost it then. It all came down on me and I lost it and I grabbed the remote bar and thumbed through several other channels and as the channels flipped by— pro wrestling, an Alan Ladd movie, William Bendix, a severely hair-sprayed man discussing Wall Street—as the channels flipped by, she moved over to her side of the bed and put her face in the pillow.

It took me two or three long minutes to say it. "I'm sorry."

"Right." She started to cry softly.

I leaned over and kind of kissed her arm. "I don't mean to take it out on you."

She kept facing the wall. "I get so damn discouraged about us when you push me away like that. You've been doing it since you walked through the door."

"I want to ask you something."

"What?" Sniffling now.

"I want to know if you'll let me inspect your underwear."

"You bastard," she said.

But she laughed. Or at least she sort of did.

Several times the next morning I thought of calling Edelman. Once I even got into a phone booth. Dialed. Waited while they put me on hold. Ready to tell him what I knew. But then I hung up and got back in my car.

In the afternoon I went into the American Security offices to pick up my paycheck.

Bobby Lee gave me some fudge that she'd made for Donna, and Diaz, the kid who'd put the choke hold on the Nam vet, gave me some grief.

In the back room, Diaz said, "You ever seen these?"

His smirk said it all. He was going to pull something out of his windbreaker pocket that was going to irritate the hell out me and he was going to love it.

172

"Diaz, I'm really not up to it today. All right?"

"Here," he said.

He brought his hand out. Over his knuckles were the metal ridges of brass knuckles.

"No more choke holds, man." He looked proud of himself. "Just these babies."

I put my hand out, palm up.

"Give them to me."

"What?"

"I want them, Diaz, and right now."

"Bullshit. They're mine. I paid for them with my own money."

I didn't say anything more. Just went over to the intercom phone and picked it up.

"Hey, what're you doing?"

"I'm going to fire you, Diaz."

"Hey asshole."

"Don't call me asshole, Diaz. You understand?" I punched a button. "Bobby Lee. Is he in?"

Diaz grabbed my shoulder. "Jesus, all right, here they are."

"Never mind, Bobby Lee," I said.

Diaz threw the knucks down on the table. They clanged.

"Enough people are getting hurt and dying these days, Diaz. We don't need to help it along."

I heard it in my voice and so did he. The same tone I'd heard in Evelyn Dain's voice. A kind of keening madness.

Diaz surprised me. He said, "You okay, man?"

"Why don't you just get out of here?" I sensed tears in my voice.

But Diaz, bully-proud in his bus driver's uniform, just stood there and said, "Man, listen, we have our arguments, but they don't mean jack shit. I mean, you're a decent guy. You know?"

I sighed. "Thanks, Diaz. For saying that."

"You let shit get to you all the time. You shouldn't. I worry about you. Everybody here does, man. The way it gets to you."

He came over and patted me on the back. "Can I tell you something?"

"All right."

"You look wasted. You got the flu or something?"

"No."

"Bad night?"

"I'll be all right, Diaz. I appreciate your concern."

But it hadn't been concern at all because as he pushed between me and the table, I saw his right hand go behind his back and lift the knucks and start to slip them into his back pocket.

I brought my fingers up and got him hard by the throat, hard enough that he couldn't talk.

"You got ten seconds to get out of here, Diaz, you understand?"

He nodded.

"And if I find you're using any weapons, including knucks or choke holds on the job, you're out. You understand?"

He nodded again.

When I let go, he said, "You need some nooky, man. Or something. You need something, man, and you need it fast."

He said this in a raspy voice. I'd dug into his throat pretty hard.

When he got to the door, he said, "Some night, Dwyer, you and me are going to face it off. You know that?"

But I didn't say anything to Diaz. He was young and hot and worried about his honor. I was thinking of Karen Lane and Dr. Evans and Gary Roberts and wondering if there was any honor left that was even worth worrying about.

30 In my apartment I cleaned and oiled my .38, checked the snap on the shiv I'd once lifted off an extremely successful pimp, and then slid on Diaz's knucks just to see how they felt. They felt good. They really did, and I knew I wanted to use them, in just the same eager bone-smashing way Diaz wanted to use them.

It was five o'clock then and I watched "Andy Griffith" on cable and wished there were a real Mayberry and Aunt Bea and Opie and Floyd the barber and Ang and Barney because I'd go down there and see them all and maybe stay a year or two. And then it was six o'clock and the news came on, AIDS and teenage suicide and crooked local politicians, and I started staring out the window at the spring rain, chill and silver on the window, and the whipping night trees beyond. And then it was seven and cable ran a "Three Stooges" episode before the ball game started, and I just sat there staring at Shemp's face, a face that even as a kid had made me sad, the gravity of the eyes, the frantic deals he tried to make with a world that needed to make no deals at all with his kind. Then I picked up Karen Lane's copy of *Breakfast at Tiffany's* and looked through it for the fifth time, hoping to find something enlightening in it. But it was nothing more than it seemed to be—the favorite book of a girl

175

from the Highlands who saw in Holly Golightly the perfect escape, the one person who seemed to do exactly what she wanted—lie, cheat, steal, care about no one but herself—and be loved for it. Holly might be fine for gentle little books and arch romantic movies, but I'd known a few Hollys in my days and they weren't forgiven or indulged forever. They were punched or even killed or they just moved on, and by age thirty-five the things in them that had been cute or fetching just looked silly and empty, and a meanness overtook them then. Go into half the bars in this town and you'll see women who used to be Holly Golightly. Now they're just drunks with evil mouths and sour memories. "She ought to be protected against herself," said a character on page 104, and I thought about that, about how Karen had needed that. And then I started wondering about the suitcase again and what was in it and thinking that maybe she was trying to protect herself with whatever it held. Then it was eight o'clock and I put a bowl of Hormel chili on the hot plate and crunched up about ten saltines in it. Then it was eight-thirty and I had two cold generic beers and went back to checking my .38 and my shiv and my knucks and knowing I was ready, knowing I needed this. Then it was nine and I went down and got in my Toyota and drove out to Pierce Point.

31 The small scarred houses of the Highlands were dark in the rain as I followed the street leading to Pierce Park. The business district came next, and even in the rain glow of neon and wet pavement it looked shabby, the windows with beer signs and the porno shops with long posters of fat strippers promising the least redeeming of pleasures.

Two blocks later I was up in the hills, driving on a two-lane asphalt road that cut through deep hardwoods. The trees looked slick with rain, as if they'd been varnished. On my right, in a clearing, I saw playground equipment yellow in the sudden jut of my headlights, and then a park pavilion with all its benches and tables piled up for winter. Nearby, I cut my lights and pulled off the side of the road, into a grove of timber, so that my car could not be seen from the asphalt. The radio was off. No kind of music could soothe me now. The rain banged on the metal roof. The windows steamed over immediately. Somewhere on the far side of the woods I could see the sprawling lights of downtown, a radio tower with soft blue lights as warning for airplanes a watercolor against the gloom. I checked everything in the big flap pockets of my green rubber rain jacket. Shiv. My .38. Diaz's brass knucks. From the flask in the glove compartment I took a long drink of Jim Beam. It felt hot in my throat but it felt good, and by the time it reached my stomach it felt wonderful. I put up the hood on my jacket and took another quick drink, not so deep this time, and got out of the car.

Where I wanted to go was a quarter mile away. I kept to the timber. The night smelled of dead wet leaves and a skunk that had been killed within half a mile or so. I could see my silver breath. The most real sound was my breathing. I carried just enough extra weight that moving through undergrowth winded me. Twice more I took hits from the flask. To keep me warm, I told myself. A dog came up, some kind of collie whose coloration I couldn't tell because he was soaked. He looked me over and apparently didn't think I was worth bothering with. He went right, deep into the timber, and disappeared. A few times I glanced up at the quarter moon behind gray clouds promising a continuation of the rain. It was a very bright moon, luminous enough to cast long shadows here in the timber. My heavy work shoes crunched pop bottles, beer cans, the plastic odds and ends left here by children playing on sunny days. Then I came to the edge of the timber and stopped, making sure to keep behind the cover of the trees. Here was Pierce Point.

Lovers had moved on to other places these days, but back in the fifties, this was the preferred spot for making out. If you were a male you came to show off your girl, and if you were a rich male you came here to show off both your girl and your car, some of the fancier ones running to chopped and channeled black '49 Mercurys, the kind James Dean drove in *Rebel Without a Cause,* or red street rods with white leather interiors and soft white dice hanging from their rearviews, or customized '55 Chevys with glass-pack mufflers that turned motor sounds into symphonies of power and prowess. The times I'd come up here with Karen Lane, we'd come in my '49 Ford fastback, and once or twice I'd had the impression that she was vaguely embarrassed by the car, as if it marked us—which it did, I suppose—as being from the Highlands, when obviously the rest of the kids were from the better areas of the city.

On the northeast corner of the Point was the edge of a cliff that was a straight quarter-mile drop to pavement below, a road used mostly by heavy trucks on their way to the power plant that squatted like a shining electric icon from a terrifying future. This was where Sonny Howard had dropped to his death.

I held my Timex up to the moonlight. In ten minutes the exchange was to take place. I had no idea how it was supposed to happen, just that it was. I sat in the cold and rain of the timber and waited. In a few minutes I'd meet Karen Lane's killer.

They came in Forester's new Mercedes.

They came right up the muddy road to the middle of the clearing and stopped, leaving their headlights on.

I got out my .38.

The rain was heavier now, almost cutting with ferocity, and in the yellow headlights it was the color of mercury.

The Mercedes just sat there for several minutes. I could see the shapes of three silhouettes through the steamy windows.

Then the driver's door opened up and Ted Forester got out. He wore a London Fog raincoat and a golf hat. In his black-gloved hands, he carried a black briefcase.

In the downpour, he walked to the center of the Point, where a formidable smooth boulder lay, a vestige of the Ice Age, and a perfect surface on which to write the name of the girl you loved. By now thousands of names must have been put on that rock.

Forester walked over to it and looked around as if he knew very well he was being observed, and then he set the black briefcase on top of the boulder that was maybe three feet wide and two feet tall.

Finally, I started to see what was going on here.

Forester looked around some more, hunching under the battering rain, and walked back to the Mercedes.

He got inside and slammed the door.

The Mercedes was put into reverse almost at once. It swept magnificently back onto the muddy road and then proceeded to back all the way out of the Point to the asphalt road, taking the warm civilized illumination of its headlights with it.

Then it was dark again, the quarter moon gone entirely behind clouds now, and there was just the rain and the smell of cold dead leaves. I took out my flask and had another belt. Not a big one or one that was going to impair me. But one I needed.

I didn't, of course, take my eyes from the boulder or the black briefcase resting on top of it.

Ten minutes passed, which surprised me.

Most money drops depend for success on speed. You get in fast and get the loot and leave.

The black briefcase was just sitting here and I wondered why.

But then when the man appeared from the east side of the timber where he'd been hiding, I knew exactly why this had taken so long.

Because he was not a man given to courage. Because he was not a man given to cunning. Because he was not a man given to success in any kind of venture, not even one like this, where he had something that other people wanted very badly.

He came moving awkwardly out of the woods on his clubfoot. He wore one of those disposable plastic raincoats you can buy for a dollar. On his head was a Cubs baseball cap and in his hand was a baby blue suitcase covered with travel stickers.

Halfway to the boulder, he tripped on something and started to fall, arms pushing out to make the fall easier, but then he righted himself and continued on.

He had no trouble making the exchange. He took the black briefcase down and opened it up and looked inside. I thought I saw him smile but I couldn't be sure. Then he closed the black briefcase and set it on the ground next to him and he took the baby-blue suitcase and set it up on the rock, and then he turned and started away.

And that's when I moved.

"Stop!" I said.

Terrified, he started moving away. I called, "I've got a thirty-eight sighted right on your back. One more step and you're dead. You understand me?"

That was all it took, that was all it ever took with somebody like him.

I walked across the soggy ground. The rain was relentless. When I reached the boulder, I grabbed the baby-blue suitcase. For a moment, it felt strange in my hand—so many people wanted this, it held the secret to so much. Then I hefted it and walked over to him.

I put the .38 right against his forehead and pulled off the safety.

"What the hell you going to do?" Chuck Lane said.

"I want to kill you."

"Jesus, Dwyer. Please. Please."

"She was your own goddamn sister."

"Dwyer, listen."

"Your own goddamn sister." I was getting crazy. I really did want to kill him.

"Whenever she needed money, Dwyer, she'd tap them. I was just going to tap them once myself. The same thing. No different from her." He was gibbering.

"Why would they pay her?"

"Because of something that happened."

"How'd you get the suitcase?"

"I went over to that spade's condo. No sweat." He sounded proud of himself.

"Why is Forester willing to pay for it?"

"You really don't know?" His spaniel eyes looked perplexed.

He had just started to speak when I heard a car come roaring down the muddy road, and before I could even turn around to confirm that it was Forester's Mercedes, the shotgun started firing.

In front of me, Lane's left shoulder exploded into

blood and shattered bone. But what was amazing was his gaze. Perfect and complete bafflement, as if this was something he could not fathom. He stared at the large red hole where his shoulder had been and then glanced up at me as if I could explain it.

I pushed him behind the boulder as the Mercedes started its circle. All they had to do was keep circling, firing from a moving car, cutting us both down.

They started on their first pass. I dropped to one knee, grabbed one wrist, steadied the gun and myself, and let go.

I got Dave Haskins, who had been leaning out the back window with a shotgun, right in the face.

For a moment, the car veered toward the trees, lights spraying over the sodden black night. All I could hear was screaming—the sounds Haskins made as he was dying, the sounds Forester and Price made at the terrible prospect of his dying.

Chuck Lane was in a pile against the boulder, unconscious. He smelled now of blood and vomit and his own feces. I reached into his belt and found a .45. I jammed it into my pocket.

The Mercedes started to back up.

I shot out both rear tires. The back end of the car sank abruptly lower.

Inside the car you could still hear Haskins screaming. That and the rain were the only sounds. After thirty seconds or so, Forester cut the headlights. I heard Price say, "Shut up, Dave! Shut up, Dave!" I had to agree with him, the dying sounds were getting unbearable. I wished I'd hit him cleaner. Then I heard the crunch: something heavy against bone. Price had shut him up, apparently crushing what was left of his skull.

Then there was just the sound of the rain and the occasional low moan of Chuck Lane.

A few minutes later the sound of the far back door opening impressed itself on the gloom even above the noise of the rain.

I didn't know which of them it was but it was obvious what they were going to do.

I got Lane by the collar and dragged him to the other side of the boulder.

Then the firing started again. It was impressive. The bullets kept coming for three or four minutes without stop and all the time the only thing I could do was hunch down and say prayers because I was so afraid. I could barely swallow and my stomach was burning all the way up my windpipe. He had an automatic rifle, maybe more than one of them. I did not want to die. I thought of Donna's advice about involving Edelman. I should have.

"They're going to get us, aren't they?"

Lane was awake again, and crying.

"Shut up," I said.

"You're scared, just like me."

"Shut up," I said again.

The gunfire had abated. I tried to listen through the rain. The leaves betrayed him and so did a furtive glimpse of moonlight.

Larry Price was circling to the east of the boulder, fanning out wide, setting himself up for some easy target practice.

I shot him once in the face and twice in the chest.

He made no sound other than falling into the leaves. A moist, final sound.

Forester called out, "Larry? Larry?" He was still in the car, sticking his head through the window.

"He's dead," I shouted back.

He had an automatic weapon too. He opened up with it and he kept up with it for two full minutes. Next to me, coming awake, Chuck started to scream.

Then I started screaming, too. I was tired of being afraid of dying. I thought of the old number about the man who was so afraid to die, he committed suicide. Only I wasn't going to give Forester that satisfaction.

I put my final two bullets into the gas tank of the Mercedes and watched it go up.

It was impressive against the night—for a moment it was hot and bright as a July noon—and you almost couldn't hear him scream and then you couldn't hear him at all, there was just the beautiful white noise of the explosion itself.

I was watching it all when I felt something bump the back of my head, and I knew that Chuck Lane was even more of a loser than I'd imagined.

"I always carry a spare, man. I'm not a dummy."

"Right, Chuck. You're not a dummy."

"I don't give a shit what you think of me, Dwyer."

He kept punching the gun into my head. It hurt. From inside my jacket I took the shiv. I eased it into my hand. Ready.

"You killed her, your own sister, man," I said.

"Bullshit. I didn't kill her. No way. I stiffed that crazy broad, Evelyn, because if she went to the cops, then the whole blackmail number would be ruined. But not my sister, man. Whatever else, she was blood."

He jammed the gun into my head again. His breath was coming in heaves that were almost sobs. "You're gonna help me to my car, man."

"Sure, Chuck."

"You're gonna help me or I'm gonna kill you."

All it took was ducking a little to the right. He got a shot off but it went wild. Just what you'd expect from a sad, desperate man like Chuck Lane.

I got him up clean, just under the sternum, and I put it all the way in and I twisted it twice, liking the sound of his surprise, and the sound of death.

"Jesus," he said.

And then I saw his face and I had to look away.

"Jesus," he said again. But he wasn't cursing. He was praying.

"You gotta help me, Dwyer," he said.

"There's nothing I can do, Chuck." I still couldn't look at him. All I could do was shake my head.

He started to cry and then he started to vomit and then he started to scream and then he just went silent. Like that, silence.

I knelt there, my back to him, soaked now, listening to the night, the rattle of rain against the trees, a factory whistle announcing a change in shifts.

The fire that had been the Mercedes was burning lower.

I got up then and walked around and stared at each one of them.

In the distance I could hear sirens.

I went back to doomed Chuck Lane, the screw-up. He was still piled up against the boulder. His eyes were open. I got down on my haunches and closed them for him and then I put my hand on his shoulder and said a prayer, a long one, and it was only partly for the men who'd died here tonight. A lot of it was for me, a whole lot of it, and what might be happening to me, the way I hadn't minded taking off Haskins' face, the way the shiv felt right and good jamming up inside Chuck Lane.

The sirens got closer.

32 "So they raped her?" Edelman asked me two hours later.

We sat in Malley's. Dolly Parton was on the jukebox. The pool balls were clacking. The rain ran like mercury down the front window. It just wasn't going to stop.

"Forester and Haskins and Price and Sonny Howard," I said. "She hung around them because she was trying to move up the social ladder, get out of the Highlands any way she could, and so she went to their parties and dated Forester sometimes and dated Price others. And then one night they all got drunk and they took her up to Pierce Point and they showed her what poor girls were really worth."

By the end I was making fists.

"You don't sound real sorry they're dead," Edelman said softly.

"I'm trying real hard," I said and without irony. "But I don't know if I'm going to make it."

He nodded to my shell. "How about another one?"

"How about six more?"

"Six more is fine by me."

So we started our way through six more, having shots brought along. "What the hell," Edelman said. "I always secretly wanted to be blue collar anyway." So he knocked back the bourbon and made a terrible face and said, "That was great."

"Right."

He sipped at his beer. "So this Evelyn thought that Karen Lane killed her cousin Sonny?"

"Right."

"Did she?"

"No. After the rape, Sonny started hanging around Karen, and he fell in love with her. He was very guilty about being involved in her rape. So guilty that Forester and the other two were afraid he was going to go to the police and confess. They were the ones who pushed him off Pierce Point. They killed him."

"You ready for another?"

"You're going to?"

"Why not?"

"I'm sure glad you got the other boys to spell you tonight."

"Let them clean things up for once. I usually get the shit detail, anyway." He signaled to Malley for another round.

I thought of what Pierce Point must look like by now. Ten emergency vehicles, red-and-blue lights startling in the gloom, the dead bodies.

He knocked this one back too, except he coughed. "Christ," he said. Then he smiled. "Being blue collar isn't as easy as it looks."

"Wait till you have to get up some morning and go punch in at some factory. Staring at stiffs sounds like fun all of a sudden."

He took a handful of peanuts from the red plastic bowl in front of him and said, "So she blackmailed them?"

"She and her brother. Over the years. Never for a lot, a few thousand here, a few thousand there. Then her brother got greedy."

"He took the suitcase. From Doctor Evans'?"

"Right."

He paused. "You going to let me see it?"

"I don't think so."

He sighed. Put his hand on my shoulder. "It's evidence."

I put my head down and thought about what I'd found in the suitcase. The story for one thing, the story she told Gary Roberts she wanted him to "touch up" for her, the story that laid it all out. Terrible writing. Confession-magazine stuff crossed with the worst sort of Holly Golightly daydreams. But it told it all—the rape, the blackmail, the brother she'd helped drag through life.

But it wasn't the story I'd remember.

It was the clothes. In the Highlands there was a tradition, brought over from the old country, and officially frowned on by the priests, of being buried with any limbs of yours that you might have had amputated during your life. I knew of an old Highlands Irishman who kept the bones of his cancer-riddled leg for forty years till he died, then he instructed his son to throw it into the casket with him.

What Karen Lane had done was not unlike that.

She'd kept the clothes she'd worn the night of the rape. All these long years later the blood soaks were almost black and the torn cotton material faded. She'd even kept her underpants. They'd been in shreds. I'd never know now if she wanted them as evidence or if she wanted to be buried with them, the way some Highlanders would want to be. I'd never know now what to think of her. She would always remain just on the outer edge of understanding, unknowable.

"I better go call my old lady," Edelman said.

I laughed.

"Just wanted to see if you were paying attention."

"Wait till I tell your wife you referred to her as your 'old lady.'"

"I'm just talking the same way everybody else here does."

I noticed he swayed slightly walking to the pay phone. I went back to my beer. I stared at all the stuff Malley sold behind the counter, combs, razor blades, breath spray, aspirin, potato chips, decongestants. He was turning the place into a 7-Eleven. Then I noticed his new hand-painted sign listing the prices for his most popular drinks, including 7 and 7s, wine coolers, pink ladies, and shell-and-shot. ("I get tired of being a frigging human menu," Malley always said.)

Then Edelman came back. "I told her I called her my 'old lady.'"

"She laugh?"

"Nope."

"You got problems, my friend."

"I told her you said it first."

"Thanks a lot."

He had some more beer and said, "One more thing bothers me."

"What?"

"Why did Karen hire you to get the suitcase?"

"Because she wanted to stop her brother from really putting the big arm on Forester and the other two. She planned to leave for Brazil next year and she wanted to put the last huge shot on them herself."

"Why Brazil?"

"It's where Holly went."

"Who's Holly?"

"Somebody who never existed, or shouldn't have, anyway."

"You're getting drunk," he said, wiggling a finger at me.

I smiled. "So's your old lady."

I spent the night at Donna's. We had popcorn and then we had underwear inspection and then we

189

watched an "Early Bird" movie called *Curse of the Vampire*, which was actually sort of scary, and then it was dawn and we slept, one of those rare times when she let me sleep touching her (she likes me to have my side of the bed and her to have hers), and then we woke up because she had to go in to the office early and so I sat in bed while she took a shower and kind of scratched myself in various places and picked at myself in others and all the time something kept bothering me, really bothering me, but I couldn't think of what it was. And then I remembered Malley's sign from last night, the one listing all the drinks and prices, the one including pink ladies, and then I recalled what Karen Lane had said right before she died; "One of the pink ladies brought me my drink." And then I remembered something else, too, so I got up and found the phone book and looked up the name of the woman who'd been checking off names at the reunion dance that night, and we had a few words of this and that and then I asked her my question and she said, "Boy, that's a weird one," but she answered it nonetheless and I said thank you and hung up fast.

Donna was still in the shower as I washed my face and brushed my teeth.

She peeked out through the curtain and said, "God, Dwyer, you're going someplace without taking a shower?"

"I figure the world can take it if I can."

"Seriously, Dwyer, you look real intense."

I sighed. "Yeah. I guess I am."

"You going to tell me?"

"Tonight. Over dinner."

She started to yell at me but she was naked and in the shower and there wasn't much she could do.

I went down and got in my Toyota.

33 It was a watercolor day, china blue sky, plump white clouds, grass greener than grass had any right to be.

I pulled in the drive and got out of the car and saw she was in back. There was laundry hanging on the line.

"Gosh, hi, Jack," she said.

"Hi."

"You probably came back for another whiff, didn't you?" She laughed. "You're getting addicted."

And I probably was. The laundry in the soft wind smelled fine and clean and made me want to be a little boy with my whole life ahead of me.

She said, "Gary was very relieved when he got home the night before. He said that everything was all right between you two." She wore a clean man's work shirt and jeans and her hair was pulled back in a soft chignon. She was everything I liked about working-class women.

"Everything's fine," I said.

She watched me and I watched her back. We both knew what I was going to say. I looked at her brown eyes and remembered that in her First Communion photograph her hair had been done in perfect little ringlets. She was female in a way as soft and seductive as the smell of fresh laundry, in just that exact way, and I wanted to hold her as I'd held her the night before, when her son had walked in on us.

She started putting clothespins on a pink blouse. She had one clothespin in her fingers and one clothespin between her teeth.

"You not going to hang your pink waitress uniform?"

She stared at me. She took the clothespin from her mouth. "You figured it out." She sounded betrayed.

"Shit," I said. The waitresses that night had worn blue. Karen Lane had mentioned a "pink lady," meaning a waitress in pink. Susan sneaking in to poison her drink.

She said, "You know the funny thing?"

"What?"

"I still liked her." She smiled, and precisely that moment her eyes went silver-blue with tears. "I probably even loved her." She put her hands out to me and I took them and felt the dampness and the roughness of laundry soap and then I slid my fingers further up to where the skin was soft and the down blond and the bones fragile as a poem.

And then I took her in my arms and let her cry and I thought of all the years I was holding here, pigtails and the mysteries of menstruation and prom gowns and hot crazed first sex and life that had borne life and the sad, silent wife she had become when Karen took away gray, failed Gary. And finally I thought of the frail frightened woman here now and I cupped the back of her head in my hand, the chignon coming softly apart, and I lifted her mouth to mine with what I hoped was reverence, and kissed her softly as I had never kissed her as boy or man, kissed her with a curious innocence as I'd always wanted to kiss her, her tears warm and salty now on lips teeth had nibbled on nervously, and I said, "You have a savings account?"

She said, "I've always wondered what it would be like to kiss you. When we used to square dance in sixth grade, I used to kiss my pillow every night and pretend it was you."

I smiled. "Did I kiss well?"

She laughed. "That's the nice thing about being in sixth grade. Everything's perfect."

I said, "I don't have to tell anybody."

"Oh, Jack. Of course you do."

"No, I don't. My friend Edelman the cop thinks that Chuck Lane killed his sister."

"But you'd know."

"I could live with it."

"No, you couldn't." She took my hand and put it to her face. Her tears were as tender as my little boy's hands when he was a baby. She smiled. "You're too much of a guilty Catholic, and so am I."

"You won't like prison."

"No, I don't suppose I will."

"So let's give it a try, all right? A secret just between us?"

She sighed and reached out and touched the laundry and brought it to her nose like a bouquet. "She would have dumped him, of course. Probably after a month or so. If even that long." She started crying again. "He's all I have, Jack. He's all I have."

I took her shoulder. Turned her around. "Susan, listen. I really won't tell anybody. I really won't."

Then I saw the line of her gaze raise slightly as somebody came up behind me.

It was her son. The one who'd caught us embracing.

He saw his mother's tears. His hands became fists. He was a Highlands boy, same as me. "He hurting you, Ma?"

"No, honey," she said. "He isn't hurting me." Then she put out her hands for him to take. "Why don't you wait here with me while Jack goes inside to make a call?"

The kid started toward us.

"You sure?" I said.

She nodded. "I'm sure, Jack."

The kid went past me, hands still fists, sneer on his uncertain mouth, taking his mother's hands gently as I had.

"You got a great mom there, kid, you know that?"

He managed to grin a little bit and said, "Yeah, that's what I heard."

I looked at her a long time, the girl of her and the woman of her, and I said, "I'm going to write you a whole lot of letters and tell you a whole lot of things."

"I sure hope you're not kidding."

I had to clear my throat because I was getting bad. I said, "I'd never kid a woman like you, Susan. Never."

Then I went in and did it. Picked up a yellow wall phone in the kitchen and dialed the Fourth Precinct and asked for Edelman and after I'd told him he said, "It never turns out for shit, does it, kiddo?"

34 That afternoon, getting ready for work at the Security company, I went to the back room and found Diaz dropping peanuts into his Pepsi, one of the more arcane rituals he practices, and tossed his knucks on the table to him.

"This some kind of trick?" he said.

"No." A few days ago I'd felt superior to Diaz and his appetites. Now I wasn't so sure.

I turned and started toward the front of the building.

"Hey," he said. "I heard all about you on the radio. Shit, man, you wasted those guys."

I didn't say anything. There was nothing to say.

Diaz grinned. "You're a hero, man. You know that?"

"Yeah," I said, "that's what I am, Diaz. A hero."

Then I went back up front and talked to Bobby Lee and asked her if she would please tell me what Elvis had whispered to her on her recent trip to Graceland, the thing that had made her feel a whole lot better.

Because that was just what I needed this soft spring afternoon. I needed to feel a whole lot better.

RICHARD STARK

"Nobody tops Stark in his objective portrayals of a world of total amorality" – *New York Times*

"A true existentialist . . . Parker conducts his business between the twin worlds of organised crime and disorganised society" – *City Limits*

Point Blank

Double-crossed, shot and left for dead in a burning house by his wife and one-time partner, Parker is out for revenge. He's also out for his share of the take, and if that means taking on the Outfit, Parker doesn't care. He's owed $45,000 and he's going to get it.

The Man with the Getaway Face

Outwitting the Syndicate means Parker must buy a new face. But once the bandages are off, keeping the new identity secret becomes a full-time occupation.

The Jugger

Jo Sheer was Parker's contact man. Now he's dead. But before he died he talked, and what he knew could nail Parker to the wall with a hundred nails.

The Black Ice Score

Stealing the African's diamonds back from the museum in the heart of New York appeals to the arch-pro in Parker, but the opposition's clumsy double-cross brings out his mean streak.

The Green Eagle Score

Parker plans to steal the entire pay roll from a US Air Force base up near the Canadian border. The heist goes like a dream, but the split turns sour.

Allison & Busby American Crime Series

CHESTER HIMES

"A crime writer of Chandlerian subtlety, though in a vein of sheer toughness very much his own" – *The Times*

"The books have lasting value – as thrillers, as streetwise documentaries, as chapters of black writing at its ribald and unaffected best. They are simply – or rather, not so simply, terrific" – *The Sunday Times*

The Heat's On

The Heat's On is one of the fastest, funniest and hardest hitting thrillers Chester Himes ever wrote. From the start nothing goes right for ace black detectives, Coffin Ed Johnson and Grave Digger Jones. Try as they might, they always seem to be one hot step behind the cause of all the mayhem – three million dollars worth of heroin and a simple albino called Pinky.

Blind Man with a Pistol

This was the last Harlem novel Chester Himes wrote. In it Coffin Ed Johnson and Grave Digger Jones are trying as ever to keep the peace, their nickel-plated ·38s very much in evidence. But this time they find themselves pursuing two completely different cases through a maze of knifings, beatings, and street riots. The risk is always that the disappearing killer and the answer to a grim problem will collide and tear Harlem apart at its bursting seams.

Also available as Allison & Busby paperbacks:

Cotton Comes to Harlem
The Crazy Kill
A Rage in Harlem
The Real Cool Killers

K.C. CONSTANTINE

"Balzic is undoubtedly the discovery of the moment" – *The Times Literary Supplement*

Always a Body to Trade

Over the years Mario Balzic has built up a precarious balance between imperfect law and practicable order on the streets of Rocksburg, P.A. But now that balance is threatened: a zealous new mayor has been elected on a "law and order" ticket and a young woman has been gunned down in the street, victim of a professional hit.

The Man who Liked to Look at Himself

Balzic has been looking forward to a day's hunting, but when it comes to it Lieutenant Harry Minyon's four-hundred-dollar bitch turns out to be a disaster. At least, until foraging in a copse, she unearths a human thigh bone.

LAWRENCE BLOCK

"Lovers alike of the American Gumshoe novel and the Great Detective novel will be delighted" – *Books and Bookmen*

Five Little Rich Girls

Five Little Rich Girls is a witty, sexy, literate and dazzling pastiche of the great American mystery novel.

The Topless Tulip Caper

Tulip Willing is a topless dancer in the Treasure Chest bar. She is also a marine biologist and tropical fish expert – a passion she shares with the great detective, Leo Haig, and the reason he agrees to help her find out who poisoned her fishfood. But pretty soon Tulip's friend, Cherry Bounce, is shot dead mid-performance, and Chip Harrison and Leo Haig know they have more than a case of food poisoning on their hands.

MAX BYRD

"Max Byrd is in the first division of American Crime writing" –
The Times

"All that we remember as best from Hammett, Chandler and
Macdonald" – *New Republic*

Finders Weepers

It all started when Leo Matz hired Mike Haller to find a prostitute who'd
been left $800,000. Within hours of taking the case Haller is framed for a
shooting he didn't do and his PI licence has been revoked. But whoever
fixed the frame-up has misjudged Haller badly, and that will cost him and
a lot of other people dear.

California Thriller

When a leading San Francisco journalist vanishes into the thin air of the
Sacramento valley, Haller is the man the editor sends for. The trouble is
someone else wants the journalist to stay lost – preferably for ever.

STEPHEN DOBYNS

"More than just a hardboiled Dick Francis, Dobyns writes real people" – *Time Out*

"Saratoga is a beguiling setting. . . . It's non-stop reading, and Dobyns gets it right" – Richard Ford

"His writing is honest, tough-minded and as uncompromising as his unforgettable hero" – Lawrence Block, *Washington Post*

Saratoga Headhunter

Ex-cop Charlie Bradshaw's new career as a private detective is progressing so quietly his successful cousins try to persuade him he should take a job as a milkman. But then one night Jimmy McClatchy turns up on his doorstep looking for a place to hide. And when Jimmy – a jockey who's turned States' Evidence in a Federal trial – winds up dead at Charlie's table, the reluctant detective's new career begins in earnest.

Saratoga Swimmer

Shortly after leaving the Saratoga police department, Charlie Bradshaw is hired as head security guard at Lew Ackerman's extensive racing stables. Ackerman has quickly become a friend of Charlie's as well as being his boss. Then Ackerman is bloodily murdered in the town's swimming-pool and Charlie makes it his final act of friendship to find out why.